A LIFE REAWAKENED

a novel

JEFF MACDONALD

ISBN Ebook: 978-1-0687898-0-9

ISBN Paperback: 978-1-0687898-1-6

*For Lorraine
my love and inspiration*

ODYSSEY

I have left all that was once me,

my backpack prepared, occupied with very few remnants of a past life.

A final turn of the key and a nod of gratitude to the haven,

which protected and offered me security behind its sturdy walls for so very long.

All evidence of a past life dismantled and left behind,

forever abandoned and best forgotten, unnoticed by those very few who pass by.

For one last time, I walk down familiar streets,

choosing indifference to the dismissive eyes of those onlookers I once knew.

I have left my land, my tribe.

My journey begins; a hooded, obscure figure, navigating territories unknown.

As I travel, I set alight the path behind me, igniting any remaining traces of a past life;

my footprints reduced to cinders and ash, kindly dissipated by the winds and rain.

Uncertainty is sighted ahead, as I enter new territories undiscovered,

but I remain steadfast, tenacious to resume my search for a new land.

The landscape unknown spreads out before me,

buzzing giants in a desolate wasteland loom menacingly above me as I travel onward.

As I enter uncharted kingdoms, my face has changed, and becomes indistinguishable;

my old, worn mask discarded and left behind in the barren ash field.

I am a stranger to those I meet;

often unseen and unrecognizable, I am a faceless entity.

I wander new paths and roads, anonymity at my side;

I am hidden and invisible, shrouded by obscurity and elusiveness.

And finally, after years of wandering, a new land appears before me.

I plant my flag, raise my tent, and begin anew.

Finally, as brisk rains fall upon me, I am cleansed and refreshed.

And as clouds slowly disappear, a new sun rises, shares its warmth, and I am reborn.

PROLOGUE

As darkness descends, I begin my run. I move through dimly lit streets, my black clothing keeping me hidden, an obscure and often unseen figure, passing quietly by those who may glance momentarily, yet take no notice as I disappear into the darkened landscape. I value the anonymity of it all, the protection of the night and the freedom to traverse familiar routes. Sometimes lost in thought, other times an observer, I find my comfort in this evening routine, which often brings calm to a frequently cluttered life.

As I run, I celebrate the moments, the liberation of constraints and expectations that too often have occupied my thinking. I value my chosen isolation; it is a time, though brief in relative terms, when I relinquish all responsibility and accountability, and am free of explanations, requirements, and the rigid structure that shapes our lives in ways we have not chosen.

I run familiar patterns, or sometimes allow spontaneity to be my able guide. This unique dichotomy never fails me, and provides the opportunity to explore, seek out, or simply enables me to celebrate the sheer pleasure of being carefree. The silence of the run is never compromised by the evening sounds of nightlife—in fact, they are often a welcome accompaniment, creating a sensitive balance between silence and sound as I wind myself through darkened streets and sleepy neighborhoods.

Running comes without restrictions, expectations, or demands. It is a solitary act that requires no investment, other than time, a solid pair of running shoes, and whatever clothing suits the season. I ignore the preachers of fitness who applaud the benefits of exercise, or the self-proclaimed gurus who clamor on about the 'runner's high' or the camaraderie of sharing this experience with others. My running only matters to me, and I seek no outcomes, other than the simple and uncomplicated experience of gliding quietly through these dimly lit streets, ignoring the needs and wants of the world around me. So, I simply ask the world, that for these very brief moments, I am left alone to choose my own pace and direction, allowing the darkened environment to become my sanctuary, my place of escape from it all.

And so I run, often without purpose or design. It is my time, and I value this pleasure of abandoning the confines that persist in keeping me boxed in. Through this very simple act, I break away from the rigid aspects of a life that can, too often, oppress and hinder.

I see a streetlamp up ahead. I hear my footsteps, my rhythmic breathing as I run along. My journey has just begun, and the night is young.

A STARTING POINT

What follows is my own story, and while in some respects it is truly remarkable, it is also somewhat bizarre and quite meandering in nature. It is not an easy story to tell, and attempting to record memories, identify key life experiences from my past, and disseminate a vast amount of information has proven to be a formidable challenge.

My ultimate objective has been to collate this information, allowing me the opportunity to bring a sense of order to an otherwise disorderly set of handwritten notes and some rather wandering, nonsensical narratives. Many of my original notes were written in haste to ensure that all details were recorded and not forgotten.

This process was intended to be therapeutic, as well as a mechanism to record and document information for the purpose of bringing clarity to a rather confusing and, at times, unsettling event that I experienced under the most unusual of circumstances. It is important to note that once this recording of information commenced, events in my life began to unfold in a most puzzling manner, which were as unique and mysterious as my original experience.

As a result of this, and after some time had passed, I was encouraged by someone very close to me, to compile all my notes, thoughts, and experiences, and turn them into a book—because, it was said, 'it's definitely a story to be told.' Ultimately, it fell upon me to shape this information into some type of narrative, and what follows is my own story and that of others—especially of one very mysterious, beautiful, and elusive individual.

Before this story can begin, there are a couple of things that must be shared, so that the stage can be set in a proper and sensible fashion. So, please forgive my rather stilted attempt at providing you with a quick snapshot of myself—however, considering the unique nature of this story, it seems like a helpful and logical starting point.

Hence, for reference purposes and as my storytelling commences, my name is Michael Lind. I am 32 years old, six foot two inches tall, and have black hair, which I cut relatively short, but not too short. I have blue eyes and am quite fair-skinned, which always makes me somewhat vulnerable to hot, sunny days. I like sports (especially running), nature, and the outdoors, enjoy reading and writing, and it is safe to say that my creative side far outweighs my analytic and methodical side—thereby making me right-brained, if one adheres to those theories.

I have always considered myself to be average-looking at best, although my mother and sister would insist differently, trying to counter my rather self-deprecating nature, saying that I had been gifted with an impressive athletic stature and very pleasing facial features. But for whatever reason, I was plagued with poor self-confidence and a timid nature from a very early age, and never quite believed or accepted the plaudits that were bestowed on me by my mother and sister. So goes self-esteem.

I was born in Chicago, Illinois, and lived with my parents, William and Charlotte Lind, and my older sister, Robyn—now 35 years old—in the Ravenswood neighborhood of Chicago until I was ten years old. Shortly after my tenth birthday, my father's work found us relocating to London, where I spent most of my remaining school years, until we returned to Chicago some eight years later.

It is important at this juncture to introduce my very good friend,

Flynn Warner, as he is an integral character in the early stages of my story. Flynn and I were childhood friends—we were the same age, and in the same grade. I met Flynn shortly after we moved to London. We resided in the same neighborhood, and were both students at Northside International, an independent school primarily established for foreign students, near our homes in Greenwich. Flynn was also American, moving to England when he was eight years old, from the Big Sky state of Montana—a result of his parents relocating to the UK so his British, and very homesick, mother could be closer to her family.

My parents chose Northside mainly for geographical reasons, as well as the fact that the school came highly recommended by some of my father's colleagues. My sister, who is about three years older than me and very extroverted, adjusted quite well to the school setting, discovering new friends, and excelling at her studies. I liked Northside, although my more reticent nature didn't help me in making friends. Northside's student make-up was very multi-cultural, and the school provided a holistic and innovative learning environment, with an array of extra-curricular activities and one independent study day at home per week.

Flynn and I managed to meander our way through the school experience without too many obstacles. We had good teachers and, over the course of our time at Northside, we both seemed to find our calling. Flynn aspired to be a painter, and me, a writer. Flynn proved himself to be an incredibly talented artist, and his skill and eventual passion were fostered by his parents, teachers, and a professional mentor. He was deemed an artistic prodigy at a very young age.

His skills as an artist were put to good use when we were thirteen years old and sitting next to each other in Mrs. Thackery's English class. Despite our best efforts at times to dissociate from her lessons—me through daydreaming and Flynn through his incessant doodling—we came to appreciate her passion for literature.

It was in Mrs. Thackery's class that we developed our first collaborative effort together: a comic strip about four space travelers streaking through the cosmos in Firestorm, an ultra-sleek and very reliable rocket ship. I wrote the stories and Flynn did the artwork. His detailed sketches of the stars and planets, and his depictions of Firestorm streaking through space, brought our wondrous tales of space travel to life. The adventures of The Firestorm Four became a favorite for many of our classmates, with each week bringing yet another chapter full of meteor storms, black holes, and space bandits. Eventually, it became a regular feature in the bi-weekly school publication, the *Northside Reader*.

It made sense that, after he left Northside, Flynn started his fast-track journey to becoming a full-time artist. He was recruited to attend a fine arts university in London and was also mentored by a successful artist who supported him and helped shape his role as an emerging young creative.

Flynn also became involved in arts movements and educational groups throughout London. This provided him with a framework to undertake his career in painting, as well as his future role as a leading advocate and supporter of various art initiatives aimed at promoting and teaching art to all who had an interest. Flynn was a true student of art and amongst his many roles, teaching others and sharing the artists' experience was, oddly enough, his very favorite.

Flynn's gregarious and outgoing personality made him naturally likable, and he was always ready and willing to enjoy the company of others. Yet if one were to see Flynn walking along a London street, his appearance might have suggested otherwise. His shoulder-length reddish-brown hair, with a full goatee and mustache, made him the true image of a Viking transplanted in modern England. His stark physical attributes—standing about six foot tall, with a stocky, muscular build—were in direct contrast to his warm and welcoming nature, which would often find him offering huge bear hugs to friends or anyone else he might meet along the way. And from this, coupled with his infectious laugh and larger-than-life personality, he cultivated a deserving reputation of being the proverbial teddy bear. It was Flynn through and through.

Flynn married his childhood sweetheart, Emily Griffin, some six years ago. He never hesitated to tell anyone that it was the best decision he had ever made in life. Emily, he used to say, more than anything or anyone, was the true inspiration behind his work. Flynn claimed that in most of his city landscape paintings, if one were to look closely enough, Emily was in there somewhere—perhaps sitting on a park bench, walking across Waterloo Bridge, or even peering out from the balcony of a Paris apartment upon the city below. She was there, somewhere—his inspiration.

As for myself, after attending Northwestern University and receiving a degree in journalism, I eventually secured a job with the North Star Media Group, working in the Chicago area. North Star owned magazines and newspapers worldwide, and had television and radio services as part of their media organization. I worked on several magazines owned by North Star, and when the opportunity presented itself to move to London to write feature articles for a human-interest monthly publication called *Narrator*, I happily accepted the offer and prepared to move back.

Upon my return to London, it was like Flynn and I had never been apart. I was supported by my employer in securing a small but comfortable flat in the Greenwich area. To my delight, it brought me within walking distance of Flynn and Emily's residence in Blackheath—the old times had returned.

So, with this brief overview, my fascinating, mysterious tale is ready to be told—and may it be said that this is no ordinary story. It is so much more. This story is a mystical adventure, a journey of self-discovery, a trip that begins in the human mind and ends in the depths of the human soul.

One last thing, if you please. As I set down my memories on paper, I made assumptions about how I may have been feeling, what I might have been thinking in such circumstances, as well as interjecting personal observations and experiences from my past. Some are accurate and factual, while others are simply assumptions. I know this must sound unusual to you, but hopefully as you read on, you will begin to understand—and everything will become clear.

As a storyteller, I felt this editorial liberty was necessary for me to truly involve you in the overall experience in a more meaningful manner. Without them, my story might lack the substance needed to help one understand the events as I remembered them. So mixed about with the memories of this event, are doses of 'reality,' so that this all might help frame the story and bring a little clarity to what was, for me, a very confusing event. I also attempted to recount conversations that I experienced in as much detail as possible.

Also, this mix of recollection and fact, supported me in the early stages of this process, to comprehend what this experience was truly about. I can only apologize if it appears confusing, but hopefully, it will help you gain some insight as to what the thoughts and feelings were that I wrestled with when attempting to record these disconcerting memories.

So, with all that in mind, let the adventure begin.

WHAT I REMEMBER

1

That day, under a bright sun, I gazed upward at a deep blue sky, experiencing a long-awaited sense of calm, as my usual wandering mind suddenly slowed, and kindly offered me a rare interlude of rest and repose. It was a radiant day, and as the sun illuminated my surroundings with a warm glow, I was given the opportunity to simply live in that moment, a welcome respite from an unrelenting mind. I was seated at a small table in Garibaldi Square in the city of Nice in southern France. A coffee and croissant on my table were the perfect breakfast on this glorious morning. The coffee seemed both desirable and needed, as a lingering sense of fatigue and the warmth of the day was robbing me of any motivation.

My reason for this visit was to conduct a search for my friend Flynn Warner, who was reported as missing in action by his frantic wife Emily. As it was, I had previously found myself at Flynn and Emily's house, when she gave me the full account of her missing husband. Emily reported that Flynn had phoned her from Nice about two weeks ago, after a trip there to meet some artist friends, not saying much of anything other than he needed time to 'sort some things out.' He had asked Emily if she might consider relocating to the south of France, buying an apartment near the port in Nice, so he could do his thing—painting, selling his art, teaching and making more inroads in the European market.

As I listened to Emily, none of it made sense to me. Emily's repeated phone calls to Flynn were in vain, coming up with nothing but a voicemail message. Emily appeared weary, from a lack of sleep one might assume, although being pregnant and still working as manager of The Family Kitchen Shop, may well have contributed to her overall washed-out appearance. Emily was a petite woman, with blonde hair, a fair complexion, and delicate, endearing features. However, her usual beaming smile and contagious laugh had instead been replaced by a sense of anguish, as she struggled to understand Flynn's sudden disappearance.

I sat with Emily in the ground-floor conservatory, or orangery as Flynn liked to call it—always with an over-exaggerated phonetic pronunciation. Even though Flynn had a designated work and studio space not far from his home, he would on occasion commandeer the orangery and create a makeshift studio, much to Emily's chagrin. Flynn's occupation of this room often continued until such time that Emily would dismiss his pleas for squatter's rights and place a very large and colorful notice of eviction upon the orangery windows.

Upon entering the orangery during one of Flynn's notorious takeovers, one might be greeted by half-painted canvasses, brushes, photos, magazines, books, paints, easels, an assortment of rags, and even a pair of his favorite running shoes thrown into the melee. But despite the hostile takeovers, the room always had a nice feel, and as chaotic as it often appeared, the space remained a sanctuary of sorts, tucked away in the far recesses of the home.

Often, when I came to visit, we would take the time to shove Flynn's 'stuff' to the sides and the three of us would find ourselves huddled together on their old but comfortable brown leather sofa, sipping on a drink and staring out into the mottled green landscape. One of Flynn's favorite paintings was of his own studio and backyard, with the colorful outside backdrop bringing a sense of contrast and calm to the cluttered, chaotic foreground. With the vibrant color of the flowers, the soothing greens, and the intricate detail of the studio—including Flynn's favorite coffee mug perched upon a paint-splattered end table—it was a vision of both complexity and order.

Emily was tearful and her voice shaky as we spoke.

"This is all wrong! None of it makes sense. Where the hell is he? I thought he wanted this life, but now I'm scared…Why hasn't he called?"

I remember Flynn telling me that after Emily fell pregnant, his focus had become making a great family life for all of them in London, staying put as he had declared. So, I had to agree with Emily—it was all very confusing, or maybe, it was just Flynn getting immersed in his work with his artist friends and losing his way, just temporarily. Whatever his reason for going missing, an odyssey of sorts began with this discussion, and I promised Emily that I would go to France, conduct this search, and hopefully solve the mystery of the vanishing Flynn. There were certainly questions to be answered.

CARVING OUT A PLAN to find Flynn seemed relatively basic, yet my not speaking French—other than a few basic words and phrases—could pose a problem. Fortunately, I was familiar with the area, having previously traveled there with Flynn and Emily during a vacation three years ago, cruising around the Côte d'Azur and eventually meeting up with some of Flynn's artist friends. I had a name and phone number for Flynn's friend Alice, whom Emily assured me spoke some English, so I felt confident this would be a good place to start.

Garibaldi Square was a spacious, colorful area, giving me a generous view of my surroundings. I remember seeing so many people scurrying about, while others sat relaxing, sipping their morning drinks. I felt an incredible sense of well-being and almost childlike fascination as I gazed outward at a passing tram filled with passengers—some reading newspapers and books, others lost in conversation, and a few just staring out, waiting patiently to arrive at their destinations. I could hear conversations around me, a pleasant blending of voices and laughter, while the familiar sounds of cups and saucers being rattled about offered up a contrasting sensory experience. I was content just sitting there, away from the life that had kept me confined for so long, too often depriving me of even the smallest and most simplistic pleasures that for whatever reason, remained frustratingly just out of my reach. It was all there—the intricacies and complexities of life in microcosm, captured in a busy and colorful French square. In this moment, I was drawn to this small but comforting corner of the world, finding myself a participant—existing within this intimate world where people came together to celebrate the art of living, rather than standing on the outside, looking in.

It was at this moment that my attention was suddenly drawn to my right—a figure walking my way, a young woman moving towards me with purpose, carrying what appeared to be a box of yellow and pink flowers. Her brisk pace suddenly came to a stop just short of my table, and after glancing over at the nearby coffee shop, her attention turned to me.

I remember that moment so well—I was mesmerized by her stunning brown eyes as she smiled at me ever so kindly.

She appeared to be about my age, and was carrying a white foam tray which held a dazzling array of pink and yellow flowers, resting inside a shallow cardboard box. She was, I had guessed, about five foot seven; she had a slight build, and was both very elegant and clearly confident and comfortable in her own body. She had jet-black hair, and when she finally turned her head, I could see a long braid falling neatly down the middle of her back. Her hair complemented her most striking face, slightly freckled with incredible delicate features. She wore light yellow shorts and a short sleeve button-down yellow and green shirt, and brown leather sandals.

In short, I was captivated by her.

Without warning, she marched forward and came to my table, and with a beaming smile asked me something in French. Her voice was wondrous, soothing and somehow reassuring. I understood her greeting, but the pace of her speech was too much and, apologizing for my lack of French, she was quick to compensate by speaking brilliant English with just the slightest hint of a French accent.

"Oh, I'm sorry. You're American." The tone of her voice was cheery; confidence was about her, and she used it well. "Can I ask a favor, please? Can I leave my flowers with you until I buy a coffee?"

Only a fool would have declined such an offer—I smiled and assured her that I would protect her precious cargo until she returned. Upon her return, she asked if she might sit with me a while, as the other tables seemed so busy on this very pleasant morning. I was, truly, lost in the moment. I couldn't believe my luck.

Once seated across from me, I noticed the attention my visitor afforded her flowers, gazing at them as if they were a prized possession. I felt it was only fair to pass comment on something that seemed so dear to her.

"Mademoiselle, I guarded them closely because I noticed a few passers-by eyeing them up."

She let out a playful laugh, saying, "Well then, I guess I owe you a debt of gratitude. Please forgive me for my poor manners—my name is Sophie."

It was at this moment that I experienced an odd sense of familiarity about her. It was a sudden, fleeting image of a time past that had been resurrected—yet one that I could not fully recollect.

It was not quite déjà vu—instead, more like the recapturing of a past moment that offered me comfort, and indeed a feeling of delight. It was there in the back of my mind, almost taunting me to remember. Yet I yielded to the logic of pragmatism, acknowledging to myself that this was strictly a chance encounter with a stranger who was looking for a place to leave her valued flower trays while she purchased a morning coffee—that was it, and nothing more.

"Nice to meet you, Sophie. I'm Mike."

"Well Mike, enchanté."

"These flowers are beautiful."

"Indeed. I bought them at the market near the promenade. They're snapdragons, my favorite. They come in different colors, but I like the yellow and pink ones best. Saying that, I do like the white ones as well."

"So, where you gonna plant them?"

"Well, in my garden of course. I have a small backyard, as you say in America, and I like to fill it with plants and flowers and just sit there amongst them all, reading my book, or just enjoying a drink in the sun."

Sophie seemed a natural conversationalist, possessing that incredible talent of creating something interesting out of nothing, and I loved it. She could have spoken about anything, and I'm sure I would have been calmed by her soothing voice, and drawn in by her alluring, mysterious eyes. I decided to tell her something about my family, to try and build a connection.

"My sister loves gardening. I was always kind of forced into having meaningful conversations with her about her plants and flowers."

Sophie smiled at this.

"So, what are you doing here in Nice? Are you on vacation?"

Oddly, I was unwilling—or unable—to explain my reason for being there. The words faded, and my response was flat and evasive.

"Well, yeah, kind of. I'm just taking some time away from work, and I like it here."

"Oh—are you here by yourself, or with family, friends?"

"No, just on my own. I'm here for a few more days, and then I'm off back home."

"Well, you've come at a good time. So, do you know anybody here?"

I couldn't help but stare at Sophie's tanned arms, and her perfect complexion.

"No, I've been here before with friends, and liked it, so I just decided to wander about on my own for a few days."

Sophie looked over at me with a pensive look on her face before she replied, "Well, I hope you enjoy your visit." With that, she looked at her watch and said, "I need to get going, as I have a lot to do today. Thanks for your company and for guarding my flowers."

"No problem—I enjoyed talking with you."

As Sophie stood in front of me, cradling her flowers in her arms, I didn't want the moment to end, but didn't know how to organically prolong it. "Happy planting, Sophie, and thanks for the company—I'll remember to make a note of your flowers. Might make for good conversation with my sister."

Sophie smiled at me and said, "Here, hold on a minute." She set her flowers down and grabbed a pen and a small piece of paper out of her handbag. She jotted something down and as I waited, I felt grateful for the time I had just spent with her. She handed me the paper and written upon it, in beautiful cursive, was the word 'Snapdragon'—but that wasn't the end of our interaction.

To my delight, she asked me out.

"I hope you don't think I'm being forward, but if you'd like to meet up tomorrow, we could have a walk around the old town and maybe go to the market."

For a few seconds, my words escaped me. But then, there was

no way I would decline such a timely invitation.

"Yeah, I'd like that."

"Are you staying nearby?"

"Just near the port. I'm staying at a guest house owned by an older woman, Madame Giron. I stayed there before with friends when we last visited. She speaks no English and I speak no French, but we seem to be getting along."

"Well then, we have a date tomorrow. I'm off to plant my flowers, and then I have my father's birthday celebration this evening, so I'll see you in the morning. Do you want to meet about ten?"

"Yeah, perfect."

"Shall we meet here? I promise not to bring any flowers with me. And hey, maybe I can teach you a few words of French along the way."

Before she left, Sophie grabbed the paper from my hand and wrote her phone number on the back. "Just in case you need to contact me."

And with that we said goodbye. As she walked away, Sophie called out to me, "Au revoir, Mike."

I turned and waved, already eagerly anticipating our next meeting. I had a date with a lovely French girl that simply came out of the blue.

It was dark now, and time for me to run. It had been this way for some time now—I'd abandoned my usual early evening runs and opted instead for late night runs, shrouding myself in the deep recesses of the night as I meandered my way through makeshift courses, enjoying the freedom of this solitary experience. I had long distanced myself from running clubs or jogging with others—my only exception being the weekly excursion with Flynn as we casually jogged around and through Greenwich Park, talking about whatever topic came to mind.

Despite my stealthy attire, I remained diligent as I ran, mindful of any dangers that lurked in the darkness. Eventually I discovered solace in this late evening routine, striding through familiar darkness, cloaked and hidden away from watchful eyes. I bought enough pairs of running shoes to fill my closet, and wore my trusty chronograph watch for the odd occasion I might time my run—if for no other reason than simple curiosity. I kept to quiet residential streets in my neighborhood for the most part, and stayed on the roads as much as possible, only using the sidewalk when the traffic left me no choice. Running became an escape of sorts, and I found comfort in it all.

I left Madame Giron's place late and ran through Garibaldi Square, around the modern art museum, back over and down to the Promenade des Anglais, and finally to the port, taking as many detours as possible. But then I was plagued by a stitch on my right side, forcing me to adjust my pace to find a new level of comfort as I ran on. My pace finally slowed, and I tried to change my breathing, but nothing worked—the nagging pain won the battle, forcing me to walk the rest of the way back to Madame Giron's, looking in at life again from the outside, listening all the while to distant conversations and laughter.

I remembered that moment so well—the observer, as I watched life happening in front of me.

As PLANNED, I FOUND myself with Sophie having a coffee near the market in Vieille Ville. It felt peaceful, and the warmth of the sun continued to ease my otherwise restless soul. Sophie's company helped too, and listening to the soothing tones of her voice was calming—although I didn't reawember too much of what was actually said, as it was mainly her smile, laughter, and charm that kept me entranced.

I remember asking her questions, lots of questions, and Sophie did her best to answer them—telling me about her present, while sharing tidbits from her past. Her childhood had been spent in Nice. Her father, an educated, self-made businessman, had founded his own company, while her mother was a schoolteacher who taught foreign languages in the local school system. Both parents had a passion for languages, and this was passed on to Sophie and her younger sister Josette. Sophie graduated from university, briefly working in Paris for a humanitarian organization before returning to Nice to work for her father. At the age of 29, Sophie said she'd found a good place in life, enjoying a calm and meaningful existence, living alone in a home with a backyard full of plants and flowers.

Oddly enough, Sophie and I were more or less the same age—our birthdays separated by only a few months—yet I certainly didn't have the same feeling of order or purpose in my life as she did.

After walking through the market, we made our way down along the Promenade des Anglais, eventually finding a bench where we sat under the warm French sun. This pitstop allowed me to ask Sophie even more questions about her fascinating life. As we talked, I felt the time had come for me to be honest, since she had been so open with me.

My rather awkward attempt to bring up my real reason for being in Nice proved more difficult than I thought—I didn't want her to think I was hiding some dark secret, only to spring it upon her later after she had been so generous in sharing her life story with me. So, I gave it my best effort.

"Anyway Sophie, there's something I haven't told you."

I was surprised to see a big smile break across her face, and after waiting a few seconds for me to continue, she finally broke the silence.

"Okay. So, are you going to tell me—are you married, or are you an international spy? I'm dying to know."

It took me some time to explain to Sophie my reason for being in

Nice, and my search for Flynn. As the details tumbled out, Sophie's expression changed to one of concern and confusion.

"I'm sorry. So, you're worried about him?"

"Well, I'm concerned. I mean it's just unusual. Flynn's not the kind of person who'd just leave his wife hanging out there like he has. It doesn't make sense. I mean, I don't think anything would have happened to him, but when Emily asked me to help her, I just felt a sense of duty to do something. I mean, he's my best friend—my only friend, really."

I took some time to further explain my relationship with Flynn, all the way from childhood into our adult lives. After I had finished telling Sophie the story of our friendship, her expression of confusion and compassion gave way to a question.

"Would you like my help? I mean if he is here in the local area, maybe I can look too."

Sophie's offer of help came as a surprise, considering we were newly acquainted, and she knew little about me, other than I was single, wrote for a living, and was searching for my missing friend.

"Look, I appreciate your offer. But you don't know me that well. Why would you be interested in helping me?"

"Well, that's a good question, I guess. And you're right, I don't know you—that's true. But I do know you like to ask a lot of questions and not answer many, that you're wandering around southern France without much of a plan, and that you were sitting alone in a French square looking like a little lost soul—but putting all that aside, you seem very genuine to me."

Sophie's brief assessment of me was pretty much on the money, and I was curious to hear more.

"When I saw you sitting there yesterday alone, you did look lost. I know that look, and I'm assuming you don't have many others in your life to help you with this. You came here on a search, and you don't even speak the language. So, I think maybe you could use a friend—a French one at that. Look, if I'm willing to put trust in you, how about trusting me? I'd like to help you with this."

For whatever reason, I was never good at accepting help from others. It had become commonplace to kindly decline, always feeling I could do everything on my own, and despite occasions when a helping hand would have been welcomed, I couldn't bring myself to say yes. Maybe it was in my DNA, but more than likely it was burned into my character, a flaw in my make-up that kept me distant from others, even when I needed them most.

It seemed like my question to Sophie had ignited in her a need to make me understand why a stranger would be so willing to help, and she wasn't about to give up.

"I know what it's like to feel alone. I've gone through those times in my life as well. So, sometimes you don't have to ask, just let it happen and let someone help you out."

There are moments in life when somebody else's logic will prevail, and in this case, I had to capitulate and admit that wandering around southern France in search of my lost friend was more of a challenge than I had considered. This was, after all, Sophie's home turf, and having her help me navigate this landscape and do the talking for me, if necessary, seemed the logical thing to do. I accepted her kind offer and thanked her for the support.

I first explained about Alice, who reportedly lived somewhere close to Nice, but said it might require some traveling to get there. Even though I'd been told Alice spoke pretty good English, I still felt it best to let Sophie do the talking. Without hesitating, Sophie phoned the number Emily had given me and asked for Alice Beaumont. A subsequent conversation ensued for about five minutes or so, and I could hear Flynn's name being mentioned along with my own. After the call ended, Sophie told me that Alice was anxious to speak to me and asked if I could come to their home near Èze, a small commune above the Mediterranean. I remembered Èze, as I had been there with Flynn and Emily when we had come to visit a few years back.

Despite feeling positive that we had contacted Alice, what Sophie had to say next was puzzling, and left me in a somewhat heightened state of uncertainty.

"Your friend Flynn is gone. He was there at Alice's but left a few days ago to meet up with a gallery owner in Nice, and Alice thinks he's left the area now. She would like to see you though, and thought maybe she could help—she's also puzzled as well as to why Flynn would go missing."

"I don't get it. Help with what? What does she mean?"

"She didn't say. She just asked if you would come."

"Well, I'm confused—she thinks Flynn has left the area?"

"She's not sure exactly. She just asked if you would go to her home, and she'll tell you more then." Sophie smiled at me. "Oh, and you don't have to do this alone. I'm invited too."

"Oh, okay. Will you come then? I mean, can you come with me, or do you want to?" I was bumbling about like a teenager asking a girl out on a first date. "I'm sorry, I didn't mean to involve you in this."

Sophie threw her head back and laughed. "I'm glad to help, and you're not taking advantage or anything. I mean, how could I miss out on this adventure anyway? She asked us to come this evening around seven."

Sophie was facing me, with her legs stretched out on the bench. I remember picking up a lovely floral scent and after mentioning it to her, she said, "It's my perfume, essence of orange blossom."

So, there we sat on a bench by the sea, listening to the waves and the chatter of those around us, enjoying each other's company.

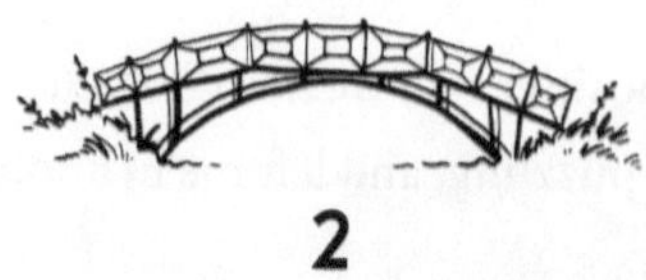

2

È ze was, as I remembered it, a small commune set above the Mediterranean, with grand views of the landscape below, stretching as far as the eye could see.

Alice and Frederic's home was picturesque, set apart and nestled into a scenic wooded area, quite far above the sea below. If one were to walk further outward from their property, they would be greeted by that incredible panoramic view below, adding yet another layer of mystique and beauty to the magical setting. I had been here before—I remembered it from my visit with Flynn and Emily. I could imagine Flynn, brush in hand, eyeing up the local scenery—in fact the scene below looked very similar to one of Flynn's paintings.

It all felt so strange, yet I was sure this was the place I remembered from my last visit. My mind was oddly cluttered, struggling with the details of the search and trying to understand my own reasons for undertaking a mission that lacked direction and clarity.

There were quite a few cars scattered about the property, and there was music emanating from inside the house. As we neared, the sound of chatter and laughter from within made it clear there was some type of gathering underway.

Alice Beaumont, in her early thirties with dark hair and a thin face, welcomed us into her home, and despite having vague memories of this place, I had no recollection of ever meeting her.

Alice blurted out at us, in her best English, "I hope you don't mind, we invited some friends and family over to help us with a local artists' project we're involved in, and well, it turned into a bit of an extended event."

Alice led us through her home, with some of her visitors staring at us intently as we made our way towards the back of the property. I felt awkward here, almost out of place, and didn't understand why Alice had asked us to come.

As we walked through the living area, London Grammar's 'Wasting My Young Years' was playing from a speaker somewhere nearby. Alice brought us to the back of the property and outside to a back patio area that overlooked a small section of woodland. It was here she introduced us to Frederic, along with her parents and brother. We were offered drinks, and Sophie and Alice exchanged some small talk, while I simply felt distracted and unable to focus on what was going on around me. I remember standing for some time, my mind wandering, distracted by the background music. I listened for a very long time as we continued our conversations with Alice's family, and then suddenly I felt an odd sense of familiarity wash over me.

Alice made certain not to leave me out. Her English was better than Emily had reported. "Flynn is a friend of ours and has been for some time now. Both Frederic and myself are artists as well. We met Flynn about five years ago when we visited friends in London. We made plans to see Flynn here, and he came out to support us with our planning. We're trying to start up an artists' retreat—we have the property and just need some ideas, so our friends and family have been trying to help."

I felt impatient, and was anxious for Alice to pass on whatever information she thought would be helpful.

"We also arranged for Flynn to meet our friend Isabelle

Laurent—she owns an art gallery in Nice. She saw some of Flynn's work from his catalog, and was taken with it, so we took him there and then said our goodbyes, leaving him with her to talk business. I'm not sure what happened afterward."

My presence only seemed to stir the curiosity in Alice and Frederic even more. Alice seemed to have as many questions as I did. "You came searching for Flynn? Sophie said you told her he was missing. What do you mean?"

I did my best to relate every detail that Emily had told me, as I didn't want anyone to think this was an overreaction on my part. Yet when I spoke about Flynn's disappearance in more detail, Alice and Frederic looked even more confused.

Alice cut me short.

"Flynn seemed fine. He didn't say anything other than he needed to get home."

"Did he phone Emily when he was here? I mean, she hasn't heard anything from him." I had to ask, as Alice seemed rather nonchalant about the whole affair.

"I guess, I don't know. But Flynn would never run away, if that's what you mean."

I didn't know what answer I'd been expecting.

Sophie tried to help, attempting to make Alice understand the gravity of the situation. "It certainly seems strange that his wife would be so concerned if there was really nothing to worry about."

I felt safe with Sophie at my side—a trusting guide, supporting me during a confusing time. Alice, by contrast, seemed frustratingly opaque. I felt at odds with the seemingly indifferent attitude that both Alice and Frederic maintained regarding Flynn's status. I also struggled to understand why she felt it was so important for us to travel to their home when they clearly had no further information or insights regarding Flynn.

I found myself struggling to concentrate once more, focusing instead on the background music that continued to play throughout our visit. The music had grabbed hold of me and wouldn't let go— what was strangest of all was that the music playing was one of my sister's playlists. Robyn loved music and would make these incredibly eclectic compilations of her favorite songs, burning them onto CDs and playing them for all to hear, or simply letting them blast out from her car's speakers, singing aloud without a care in the world. One of her playlists was a mixture of old and new—The Crystals, Elvis, The Hunts, Taylor Swift, Buddy Holly, Van Morrison, Norah Jones, Imagine Dragons, The Foundations, and more—fused together in a musical menagerie. I received a copy of this CD from Robyn as part of a small care package that she sent my way some time back.

During our visit to Alice, songs from this compilation continued to play. Even Marvin Gaye's 'Inner City Blues'—placed in Robyn's compilation at my request—had come up as we were speaking with Alice. How could that be? Who other than Robyn would have compiled this eclectic mix of music? I couldn't bring reason to it all, yet it was there, playing on, challenging me to rationalize a very irrational moment in time.

The music drew me inward to the back entrance of the house, and I found myself standing at the back of the living area, seeing people but no faces, listening to my sister's playlist as it mingled with the indiscernible French conversations continuing throughout the room. I suddenly felt anxious and uncomfortable, wanting to leave this place behind and all the frustration and confusion that was swirling about in my head. I excused myself from the group and walked back through the house, passing by their guests without taking notice of anything as I made my way outside. I stood alone in the warmth for a few moments, bewildered.

It was only when I felt a hand on my back and the lovely voice of Sophie that I was able to regain any perspective about where I was. She looked at me with a concerned expression, maybe trying to understand what was happening to me.

I stumbled with my words as I explained to Sophie the best I could.

She was intent on giving me an explanation, saying, "Just a weird coincidence, I'm sure."

"How could that be? I know this music, these songs—my sister compiled this playlist."

I could see Sophie struggling to find the right words.

"I think you're just worried about your friend. It all seems kind of mixed up. Maybe just be a little patient and I'm sure it will all become clear."

We returned to Alice and Frederic and thanked them for the invite, explaining that we needed to go. I had to see Isabelle Laurent. Alice provided us with Isabelle's contact details, and I thanked them again for meeting with me. It was only once outside that I felt Sophie's hand in mine. I came to a sudden stop, as The Seekers' classic song, 'I'll Never Find Another You'—one of my sister's favorites—rang out.

I stood for a moment and looked back at the house, mystified by my visit and the music. Sophie pulled at my hand, urging me forward, knowing maybe I needed to move on from this place.

BEFORE SOPHIE SAID GOODBYE for the evening, she kindly contacted Isabelle Laurent and made plans for the three of us to meet for lunch at a restaurant in Nice the next day. I was grateful to Sophie for her dedication to the cause, yet I felt a sense of guilt for dragging her along on what had begun to appear like a wild goose chase. Sophie assured me that she was glad to help and informed me that Isabelle spoke very little English, so her role as translator could prove useful in uncovering any further information about Flynn's whereabouts. There was no way to argue with Sophie's logic, so I once again accepted her help, also knowing all too well that this may be the last time I would be in her company.

Once inside my room, I sat on the bed, feeling awash with fatigue and uncertain about our search for Flynn. I was exhausted and the confusing events at Alice's house didn't help my situation. Despite the relentless fatigue, my mind was in high gear, with images of my sister mixed in with the unsettling experience at Alice's. The constant feeling of having no control of my situation and losing my bearings along the way left me anxious, so I decided a run might help clear my mind.

I found myself running through central Nice, heading north. The air was warm and humid, and again I felt a sense of detachment from my surroundings, all the while fighting a relentless and unforgiving stitch on my right side that continued to stifle the enjoyment of my runs. Despite the pain, however, I ran on and on, paying little attention to where I was or taking notice of any physical landmarks that might help guide my way back.

My pace quickened and I suddenly seemed able to tolerate the pain, increasing my speed even more as I ran on. For the first time in a while, I ignored the menacing sense of desperation that seemed to follow close behind, and I simply ran—nothing but running and running even more, not caring where I was or who was around me.

I just ran.

Suddenly, and out of nowhere, a jarring jolt of reality seemed to realign my senses and I slowed my pace, trying to figure out where I was. It was dark out, very dark, and I found myself in an unfamiliar neighborhood. I was lost, and quickly became gripped with anxiety. My attempts to survey the unknown surroundings yielded no evidence as to where I had ended up. Street names meant nothing, and panic and fear had taken hold, heightening my sense of disorientation even more. I started to run fast and kept my pace up, hoping to find a way out of this maze of roads.

As I ran on, I felt as though I was running from something that was menacingly close behind me, and though I was nearing an outright sprint, the dark streets and dimly lit homes offered me little protection from this imagined pursuit.

Finally, after some time at a desperate, heightened pace, and unable to free myself from the intense anxiety I felt, I somehow found my way back to Garibaldi Square. The relief of finding my way back brought me an immediate sense of calm as I slowly walked my way through the square.

This experience, though brief and irrational, had left me shaken and without explanation.

ISABELLE LAURENT WAS A stylish woman in her early forties and owned Galerie Rouge, an art gallery situated in central Nice. Sophie and I were seated across from Isabelle in a small restaurant located on a trendy side street near the gallery. As Sophie had said, Isabelle's English was not great, and once we got down to the business of Flynn being missing, I felt exasperated sitting back and having to feed Sophie questions, before listening to their ensuing conversation without a clue as to what was being said. At times, the conversation between Sophie and Isabelle seemed to take on a life of its own, and I wondered silently what else they could be sharing.

I soon found myself distracted again by the lovely scent of Sophie's perfume, as the sweet fragrance resurrected a memory and image from my past. It was a strange feeling, and I found it difficult to concentrate once again, baffled by the intrusion of a memory long past.

Isabelle tried to look over at me when she spoke, but it was Sophie's translation that I wanted to hear. After a few minutes of conversation between the two of them, Sophie turned to me with the update I had been waiting for.

"Isabelle said that Flynn was here, but only for a couple of days. They talked art and she was interested in some of his work, and then he left and headed off to Paris, to meet a woman by the name of Gisele Dubois."

I knew that name. I had met Gisele Dubois when she and her husband stayed with Flynn and Emily in London for a few days a while back. Also, on our way back from southern France, the three of us stopped in Paris and met with Gisele at her gallery.

In the end, there wasn't much more I could gather from Isabelle. She tried to be as helpful as possible, but couldn't add much, other than saying there seemed to be nothing out of the ordinary going on with Flynn. He was just doing the rounds in France and meeting up with some of his artist friends. So once again, I was seemingly a step behind, but now I was even more determined to find my lost friend.

Isabelle said that Gisele owned the Loft Galerie in the 4th arrondissement, and I was certain, as she described it, this was the place I had visited with Flynn and Emily. I hoped the visit with Gisele might bring an end to my rather fruitless search—or, at the very least, provide me with some answers on which to go on.

THAT NIGHT, I SAID goodbye to Sophie and Nice. I felt at a loss in so many ways, as Sophie and I sat in a small café in the old town talking about our time together and the strange and frustrating search for Flynn. I felt a sense of sadness as I looked over at her. I thanked her for all she had done and promised her that when I returned home to London, we would make plans to meet up again.

Sophie looked over with a slight smile on her face. "We were just getting started. So, listen here, we don't like to say goodbye in France—it's not good enough. That is why we say 'au revoir.' It means goodbye, until we meet again."

It was difficult for me, sitting there, confused by Flynn's disappearance, and having to quell the profound sadness that swept over me as I looked into Sophie's eyes. I remember studying her beautiful face, not wanting that moment to end, and with that came an incredible impulse to stay there, abandoning all that I had for a new life in France. But it was simply an impulse, a ridiculous one at that, as reality demanded I do the responsible thing and return to my life back in England.

So, for those few moments, as we sat in that intimate café at our small corner table, I felt comforted by Sophie's presence, and was thankful for her willingness to help a stranger in need, as he desperately attempted to navigate his way through a very confusing landscape.

As we looked over at each other, I remember Sophie saying, "We will find each other again, when all this mystery has faded away."

With that she smiled, and I could feel her hands in mine. I gazed upon her beautiful face one last time, before we parted ways. But it was time to go, and figure out what I was searching for.

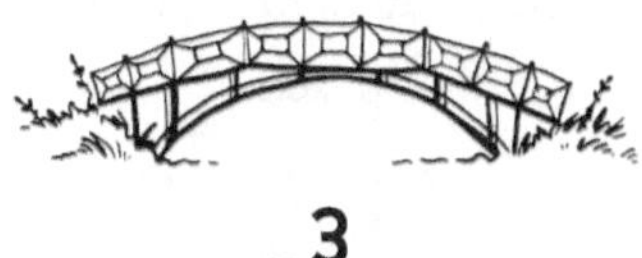

3

Standing in the center of Paris was like retracing my steps from my previous journey here, as Flynn, Emily and I came to this exact spot after leaving Nice just a few years before. I was near Notre-Dame, having made my way to the general vicinity of the Loft Art Gallery, where I was to meet up with Gisele and her husband Alex.

Upon my arrival, I was greeted by the outgoing and smiley Gisele, whose distinctive and warm personality was well-matched by her striking physical appearance. At five foot seven or so, with long, wavy red hair and a face full of freckles, combined with a lively personality, Gisele was one of the most gregarious individuals one could ever meet. Her dress sense was exotic and bright, and with a warm and lively personality to match, it was easy to become drawn in by her. Both Gisele and Alex were in their mid-forties, and each had a deep passion for, and commitment to, the world of art. It was easy to understand why Flynn was such a good fit with the two of them—similar personalities and levels of enthusiasm that would inspire even the most reluctant to share in the experience of the artists' way.

As we said our hellos, both Gisele and Alex were just as I remembered them. Clad in a white dress, adorned with bright blue and red flowers and wearing red shoes, Gisele's attire was all the perfect accompaniment to her flaming red hair and exuberant personality. Alex, the more conservative of the two, was a congenial individual, always ensuring that those around him were made to feel comfortable and welcome. Flynn had met Gisele and Alex some years back, at some point along the artist's path. The gallery, however, wasn't what I remembered.

As Gisele and Alex led me to their main office, tucked far away in a quiet back corner of their gallery, I was suddenly drawn to a painting hanging on the far wall. It was a copy of an original painting that Flynn had created, a gift to me on my twenty-seventh birthday. Flynn called it 'Stargazers,' and it depicted a man and a woman standing on a bridge facing outward and staring up at a starry sky, with a bright cityscape off in the distance. There were also a few silhouetted figures passing by on the bridge, with a dull lamppost casting just the right amount of light upon the couple looking upward. Flynn said the man on the bridge was me, but when questioned as to who the woman was, he replied that, at the time of painting, her identity remained a mystery and that it was for me to figure out. Flynn was always a funny guy, and we had a good laugh about it all. The original was proudly displayed on my living room wall.

Gisele's words only deepened the mystery even more.

"We have a few of Flynn's paintings here."

"I know this one," I said without hesitating. "It was a gift from Flynn. Just seems odd to see it hanging here."

Once seated inside Gisele's office, she no longer kept me in suspense.

"Flynn was here, but only for two days. He left about three days ago." Both Gisele and Alex stared at me, and possibly saw the disappointment in my face. "Does he know you're looking for him? Have you phoned him? This doesn't make any sense."

Gisele's questions seemed redundant, and I didn't know how to answer them, or if I even wanted to, but I did my best.

"Emily said he left to meet up with some artist friends in Nice, but only for a few days, and was then due to return home. But when I met with his friends in Nice, they said he had left to come here. I can't even follow the timing of it all, where and when he traveled. Emily is a mess with all the worry."

Gisele looked bewildered.

"Flynn didn't say anything to either me or Alex. Just said he had to make it back home. Everything seemed alright. We just caught up on life and he talked about the baby and all."

The three of us sat for a moment in silence, seemingly puzzled by everything. Why did I keep missing him, and why did the relentless frustration of the search leave me even more confused than before?

Gisele looked as though she was contemplating a deep mystery, before saying, "One more thing you should know. Flynn was flying over to Michigan to spend time at his brother's house before heading home."

I wasn't sure I heard Gisele clearly.

"What? His brother Sam lives in Norfolk in England, not Michigan. And all the way to the US before returning home…I don't get it."

"I know it must sound confusing, but he said his brother recently moved to Michigan for work. Flynn said he was going for a quick visit. Maybe he wanted to get everything in order before the baby comes along."

Gisele grabbed a small spiral notebook and thumbed through it until she found where Flynn had written down his brother's new address. When I saw the address, it felt like a lightning strike, and as I tried to gather my senses, disbelief crept into the room and left me at a loss to understand any of it.

Flynn's brother Sam had moved to Aston, a small village in Michigan's Upper Peninsula, and I knew it all too well—it was only about ten miles from Westfield, my father's hometown. How was it Flynn never told me about this, and why would Sam move to some small town in Michigan's Upper Peninsula? And why would Flynn travel all the way to the States for just a short stay, instead of returning home to his pregnant wife? Why did he jot down his brother's details in Gisele's notebook? The questions kept coming, and I felt like I was chasing something elusive and seemingly out of reach—tormenting me, yet pushing me to carry on despite my better judgment.

Gisele did her best to offer me some reassurance.

"I think Flynn's going to end up back at home, so I wouldn't worry. He's well grounded, so maybe he's just having a bit of wanderlust, is all."

As with Alice Beaumont, I was surprised by Gisele's indifference to Flynn's situation. Flynn left his wife and home for a short visit to France, and since then, his missing person status and unwillingness to answer any phone calls did not seem like some casual bit of wanderlust. There had to be something more to all of this. I said my farewell to Gisele and Alex, and despite wanting to give up my search, I had come too far to stop now. There had to be something more to Flynn's desire to go AWOL, and it was certainly not rooted in some desire to avoid his marital responsibilities and head off traveling without keeping his family in the loop. It just wasn't Flynn, and for that reason the search for my globetrotting friend would continue.

It was time to move on—Michigan was waiting.

I walked from Gisele's gallery into early evening Paris life. The streets were electric with big city energy, full of light and noise as people walked about, navigating their way to whatever destinations had been calling their names. It was warm out, and as I walked on, I felt weary, plagued by the relentless fatigue that clouded my thinking, forcing my mind into overdrive, as I tried to make sense of

Flynn's desire to go astray in such a bewildering manner. I continued walking with little purpose or destination of my own, losing my way as I meandered through the streets of Paris—an isolated figure cast against the backdrop of a city teeming with life. This search for Flynn had led me here, and what started as a layman's attempt to find a misplaced friend, had now taken the shape of a legitimate mystery.

I had even considered the possibility that maybe this was an escapade of sorts, some odd plan hatched by both Flynn and Emily to drag me out of my own repetitive stupor. But that seemed rather unlikely.

The reality seemed to be that Flynn had decided to travel away from home, cutting off his family and closest friends, leaving his nervous wife and the rest of us to wonder what could have possessed him to do such a thing.

At least the search had brought something good and hopeful to me—a young French woman who had walked into my life and kept me entranced as she regaled me with stories about flowers and what life was like in sunny southern France. As my mind wandered and thought of Sophie, I imagined her looking over at me across that small table in Garibaldi Square, her face beaming with that lovely smile and asking me in such a loving way if I would kindly walk her home.

Maybe that would happen one day, but for now I remained grateful for that fortuitous meeting between two strangers—when, for just a moment in time, I had been offered a hopeful glimpse of a life yet to be discovered.

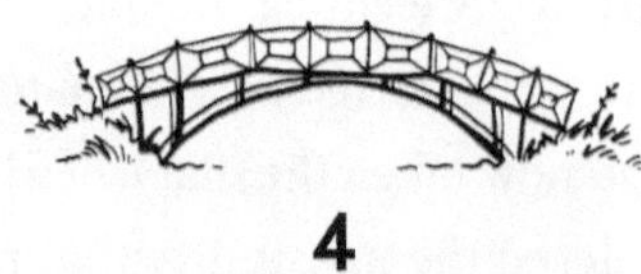

4

Aston is a sleepy village located in the far west of Michigan's Upper Peninsula. As a child, I was fascinated by the fact that, traveling to my father's hometown, we would leave the eastern zone and travel back in time an hour into the central time zone. When I was twelve years old, I even wrote a short story about a boy who saves the world by traveling to his aunt's house on the far western tip of the Upper Peninsula, since he's able to gain an extra hour. If life was only that easy and convenient, gifting us those opportunities to go back and undo those times and moments when we made poor decisions or chose behaviors that resulted in shame, upset, regret, or even tragedy. But as a twelve-year-old wannabe writer, saving the world made more sense than undoing one's past mistakes.

The Upper Peninsula, or the UP as it is often referred to, is always raved about by those who live there. A few smaller-sized cities are spread throughout the UP, but it mainly consists of small towns that offer a true glimpse of this beautiful land. In between these towns and villages is forestland, waterfalls, scenery, wildlife—in other words, calm. Michigan's nickname, 'The Great Lakes State,' comes from it being the only US state that borders four of the five Great Lakes. Both my parents' families originate from the UP, and there was never a visit in my childhood when I didn't hear 'you're in God's country now' from some family member or other, telling stories of great deer hunts or the satisfaction of a night's smelt dipping shared with good friends.

There's a charm to living in a place where life still moves slowly enough for a person to find satisfaction in reading about the birth of a newborn baby in the local gazette, or gathering at the local tavern for a burger and beer while sharing in the neighborhood gossip. It's also knowing that the biggest traffic issue you might run into is waiting somewhere on US2 as a family of geese or deer make their way across the road. On some starry nights, the Northern Lights dance away, entertaining those who might brave the cold to catch a glimpse of this stargazer's delight.

I was at Sam's house, bemused by the fact that he had somehow found his way to this remote and sleepy corner of the UP. I had been to Aston with my parents on many occasions as we passed through en route to my father's hometown.

Sam was Flynn's younger brother by two years. He was an IT consultant, had been married to his wife Jenna for about three years and they had a two-year-old son, Freddie. Sam was home alone, and after seating ourselves in his living room, he informed me that he moved to Aston just recently, securing an IT post with a local engineering firm that worked throughout the UP.

Sam spoke in a genuine and straightforward manner about his reasons for moving to Michigan.

"It was a change me and Jenna wanted, and we really like it here, so here we are."

Sam was aware of my history, and knew that this was my father's homeland, but we only discussed it briefly before moving on to discuss Flynn's disappearance.

"He was here for about three days, but was desperate to get back to London."

My confusion must have been evident, as Sam looked at me with a quizzical look on his face.

"He came all this way for such a short visit? Did he go somewhere else?"

I felt desperate to make Sam understand my own frustration in attempting to conduct this makeshift search, but I felt as though I was fluttering about in the wind, unable to bring any logic to the situation.

"Emily came to see me and asked for help. He's been missing and nobody's heard from him. I went to France to find him, but I just kept missing him."

"He just said he was away for a while doing some business, and that he needed to get home. We didn't talk much about it."

"What did you guys do when he was here?"

"Not much. Talked, took him fishing, ate, drank—did what anybody else would when they meet up with family."

None of it made any sense to me. Why was everyone acting so casually about Flynn's flight of fancy? Emily was so full of certainty that something was wrong, but was it all an overreaction? And was I destined to always be one step behind him?

Despite acknowledging that Flynn's dismissive attitude about straying from home was, at the very least, puzzling, Sam seemed keen to assure me that Flynn's state of mind was fine and that there didn't seem to be anything out of the ordinary going on with him.

"Flynn went home to his wife after he left here. That's all there is. There's no mystery here—when you meet up with him, I'm sure it'll all become clear."

Before I left, I had to know more about Sam's move to Aston.

"Why here, Sam? Why Aston? How did you even know about this place?"

"Well, life takes some unexpected turns. When I accepted the job, I didn't think we'd end up here. But here we are."

My conversation with Sam ended on that note, leaving me even more mystified than before. I was none the wiser about Flynn—yet maybe somewhat relieved to know that all was not lost, and that maybe he was home by now.

TEN MILES FURTHER WEST of Aston is the very small town of Westfield. A set of railroad tracks marks the edge of town, and the town consists of a gas station, two churches, a grocery store and a few other shops dotted along their main street. My aunt Jenny, my father's youngest sibling, lived in a two-story house with her husband Robert. Her only child, Rochelle, was married, had two children of her own and lived nearby.

Aunt Jenny was home alone, and we sat in the kitchen at the long oak wooden table that had held up remarkably well over the years. Jenny smiled at me as she placed a glass of her homemade lemonade in front of me. My father loved her lemonade, and when we use to visit, we never left without a homemade meal and a glass of her favorite drink.

"Been a long time Mike, thought you forgot about us here. Last time I saw you was when you all came to bring your daddy's ashes. We've missed you."

It felt like an eternity since my mother, Robyn, and I made the trip back here to spread my father's ashes near Hendon Forest on the shores of Honovi Lake—though the two of them usually made the trek up to the UP every year to visit. My mother was born and raised in a small mining town called Aurora, about an hour or so east of Westfield. Her family still lives there—a few siblings, nieces, nephews, and cousins, plus many friends and acquaintances from her younger years.

I was at a loss as to what to say to Jenny, as I had avoided this place for fear of facing those memories all over again. It became all too easy to hide away in the big city and get on with life. City life had become a haven for me—safe, tucked away, and camouflaged amidst all the chaos of fast-paced, modern living.

"You know, your dad was so happy when you all came to visit. He used to take you and your sister trekking through the woods, looking for whatever wildlife he could scare up—do you remember? Never went anywhere without that camera of his—taking pictures of the trees, sunsets, and the old train mining cars that used to pass through. He loved it all. Whatever happened to that camera, anyway?"

"Well, I've got his old Canon, but I'm not sure where the others ended up. I think maybe my mom still has them."

That camera of my father's, which was passed on to me by my mother, is one of the few prominently displayed possessions on my living room shelf. In some respects, it is a reminder of my lifelong desire to create, mainly through writing and photography. My mind has always been an ongoing visual collage of images, stories, and even tales of wonderment. From an early age, photography captured my attention, as we would spend many nights viewing my father's splendid slideshows of rivers, lakes, snow scenes and anything else he'd captured while out on one of his nature expeditions. I loved it all and when I was old enough, I was gifted a camera—thus my own journey started. When I began my journalism studies, I initially considered photojournalism, but my desire to write, report, and create stories was a powerful calling, so my interest in photography became relegated to the hobby category. However, I never lost the passion, and to this day my camera is always within my grasp, ready to capture those special moments.

When Jenny smiled, she looked a lot like my dad.

"We always have a good time when your mom and Robyn come through. Last year, we drank a little too much of your Uncle Robert's homemade wine. Oh, we had a good laugh together. We all make it to their place in Chicago on occasion. It's always nice being with them."

"So, where is Uncle Robert?" I asked.

"He took Rochelle and the kids over to the decorating store in Handley. Rochelle and James bought a new place over on Webber Street, and your uncle is helping them renovate it."

My feeling of disquiet had returned with a vengeance.

"Mike, you look like a little lost boy—why don't you stay for a bit?"

I couldn't stay, and so needed to get repositioned somehow. This was something Flynn and I used to joke about when we used to skip school together, and knew our parents would be far from happy if we got found out. We discovered the word 'repositioned' and used it when we had to deal with a difficult or uncomfortable situation.

"Why don't you go to Hendon, take a walk to the lake? Seems long overdue."

I explained to Jenny why I'd ended up in her kitchen. The mystery of Flynn's disappearance seemed to intrigue her, and she sat for a few moments in contemplative silence before responding.

"Maybe, it really isn't a mystery at all. Maybe his wife just lost sight of things because she's pregnant and got all worried. Besides, sounds like he's gone home from what you said, and it seems like you're the one who needs to find his way back."

I could only nod my head, and after saying my goodbyes and promising to pay a proper visit in the future, I made my way out of there.

As I stared out at Honovi Lake, trying to enjoy the pleasant temperature, I wasn't sure what to feel. I had stood here with my mother and sister and scattered my father's ashes so many years ago now. It was cold that day, and we stood for about an hour, until my mother wanted to go. We didn't speak much, and both my mother and Robyn wept before going quiet. I can remember that day clearly, standing and looking out at the lake, feeling angry and struggling to understand why life turns out the way it does sometimes. I couldn't find the words, and my father's loss left me feeling empty and unable to make any sense of it all.

Life has its tragic stories; they are out there, all around us, and they just don't happen to other people.

I couldn't console my mother and instead left it to Robyn, knowing that time would move on, and eventually we would all get on with living—no matter how difficult or challenging it might be.

Robyn was the one who began to fill the void in my mother's life again. Grandchildren, family events, and vacations—Robyn became a lifeline for my mother, and even though I convinced myself that I hadn't dropped out of sight, I had indeed hidden myself away from it all. I distanced myself from them, and living in London provided me with a comfort zone, having left behind all that I once knew. My mother and Robyn nagged at me constantly to participate in family life, but so often I found myself sitting on the outside looking in, and sadly not knowing how to find my way back. Such was what my life had become.

As I stood alone, looking out at the lake, I felt that sense of emptiness again. I tried to never think about my father's death, as it was simply too tragic. And even though some odd twist of fate brought me back here, I still refused to peer any deeper into it all than I had before.

That night, I ran through Westfield. It was dark and the roads were quiet; I listened to the sounds around me, but heard very little. At one point I thought I could hear people talking, but could not see them because of the dark. The pain from my stitch was better, but still lingered. It was a strange feeling running in the dark, as there were moments when I couldn't sense I was even moving—as if I was running in place.

I ran on and on, following the same route over and over, running without much purpose—an exercise in futility. This search for Flynn had brought me back to places I knew and things that I was once familiar with. It was an odd journey, one that had not yet reached its conclusion.

As I ran on, I could hear Sophie's voice again, softly repeating to me what she said upon my departure from Nice: "We will find each other again, when all this mystery has faded away."

It was time to keep moving.

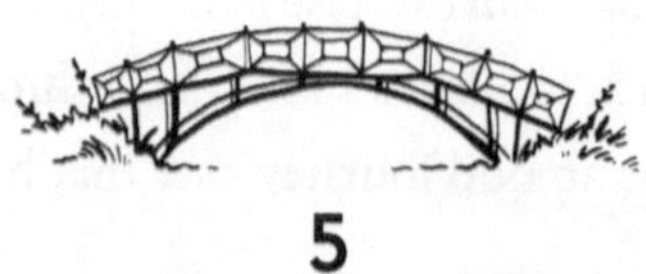

5

I was standing at Flynn's front door, but despite my incessant attempts to make myself known, there appeared to be nobody home.

Out of desperation, I made my way to the backyard and grappled with the unyielding fence, finally managing to get a peek at the darkened orangery. But this offered me no clues as to Flynn and Emily's whereabouts. I waited out front for some time, even looking for a neighbor who might provide me with something to ease my anxiety, yet nobody was forthcoming.

Once back in my apartment, feelings of isolation began to unsettle me, and having nobody to speak to about the missing Flynn put me in a restless state. I was at a loss as to how best to bring meaning or understanding to anything. The maze of uncertainty seemingly offered no way out, and I felt encased by an overwhelming feeling of desperation. The countless obstacles, not to mention the abstract and confusing images and thoughts that had resulted from this mystery, were preventing me from locating my missing friend. I didn't know how to move forward, how to escape this limbo I was living in.

In some respects, the search for Flynn had become secondary, and instead it was my own isolation and detachment from those around me that began to take center stage. Was this even about

Flynn? I couldn't be sure any longer, and thinking back on the search, I had slowly become haunted by the same images—Flynn's disappearance, my father's life and death, my sister Robyn, and my own place in life. It was all there, part of this mystery in some sense. I had become suspended, stuck in one place, unable to find my way out of it all. A lost soul trying to find his lost friend. My apartment had a peculiar feel to it—silent, unlived in, and lacking any warmth and comfort. Where was everybody?

I needed to find Flynn and Emily, and ask what had happened— why he disappeared in the first place, and left those closest to him behind to unravel this peculiar mystery.

It was time to return to the darkened streets, and run to escape my troubles.

Running had become my liberator, my safe place, yet on this night, dark and haunting forces ran alongside me. I struggled to find that peaceful and restful place that would so often offer me comfort, and before long, I was awash with grief and sadness.

The constant weight of despair pushed at me, forcing me to cut my routine short, leaving me to seek emotional refuge on a park bench. As I sat with my head down, without warning, the full impact of grief was unleashed upon me, grabbing hold of my vulnerable soul and leaving me exposed to the harsh emotional elements that were slowly tearing me down. As strong as I had once been, never wavering, never conceding to these persistent and negative forces acting upon me, and despite a sense of desperation to find my way out, I was unable to fight back, surrendering myself upon a weathered park bench, as any hope of resolve trickled away into the darkness.

Once back in my apartment, I was finally able to settle myself. As I sat back, I thought of Sophie again—that unusual encounter that became the starting point for a search that had not yet concluded.

Sophie had reached out to me when I needed somebody the most, and as I thought of our time together, I promised myself that I would find her again when this strange and twisting search would finally come to an end.

I OPENED MY DOOR to Emily Warner, who stood silently before me, her rather inscrutable expression offering little as to the mystery of her missing husband. So many questions came to mind, yet I jumped in before she spoke and rambled on about my search for Flynn.

After my rather lengthy explanation, I was finally able to compose myself.

"Emily, what's going on?"

Emily appeared expressionless and answered cryptically, "Flynn's back, and he's fine. Everything's good."

I attempted once again to explain my frantic search, but then simply asked, "Where is he? Is he home?"

Emily spoke with an edge of certainty in her voice, but offered little as to what happened with Flynn.

"Mike, I think you need to ask Flynn those questions. Everything's alright, trust me. But you need to see him and talk with him. He has things to tell you."

My confusion only deepened thanks to Emily's vague responses.

"Where's Flynn? I was at your house, but neither of you were there."

"It's all good. I'm sorry for the bother I caused you and for all that you went through. It was just a misunderstanding, that's all." Emily's facial expression remained unchanged, and the level of frustration I was feeling continued to grow. "He's meeting with his friend Jeremy from Studio K, and a few others in London right now. Do you remember Jeremy? Flynn asked if you could meet him there at St. Joseph's church in North London, on Riffington Road. He said you'll know where it is, near Blackwell Road. There's a meeting there that he thinks you'll be interested in."

"I don't know that church and I don't know any Jeremy. Blackwell Road, that's where Julia's parents live. I don't get any of this. When is he home? I'll just wait till he's back."

"Please go now, he's waiting for you. I think he wants you to be a part of this meeting."

"There's no church on Riffington Road. I know that area well, and it's just a residential street. Can't you just tell me where he's been?"

Emily's expressionless look remained, and she offered me no further information, repeating her request for me to travel to North London as per Flynn's request.

"I think everything will become clearer once you see him."

With that our conversation ended, and I was no closer to understanding Flynn's sudden absence than I was before. I hadn't been to that area of North London for a very long time, but if that was where Flynn had positioned himself, then that was where I needed to be.

I WANDERED UP AND down Riffington Road, but there was no St. Joseph's to be found—no church at all for that matter. I stood, clad in my running attire, waiting for what—I was no longer certain. It was dark out, and there was an unsettling quiet to the area—a street without life. I assumed most people were tucked away inside their homes, distancing themselves from the world outside of their front doors. There was a big part of me that wanted to give up the fight; I was tired of trying to make some sense of something that was completely irrational in so many ways. Why did it matter any longer? If there was a larger family issue at play, then that was something

Flynn and Emily would need to work out between themselves. Why was I even there, standing in the dark?

After some time, I found myself on Blackwell Road. Across the road, and two houses down, was the Watts family home. This is where my ex-partner Julia and her three very successful siblings had lived with their parents, John and Marilyn Watts. I had been there on several occasions with Julia for family events and holiday celebrations. The home appeared dark and desolate, and I waited, hoping to see someone either come or go. Maybe Julia was there, visiting her parents, and so I continued to stand and stare, my eyes fixated on the house, not wanting to leave for fear of missing out on some significant event or happening. But what? What was it that I would be missing? What did I expect to happen? Maybe a chance to say something to Julia, to say I was sorry.

How and why things ended the way they did must have been rooted somewhere in my psyche—more than likely the result of something that kept me distanced from those around me. So why would I take such a risk and try to speak to her?

Instead, I stood rooted to the spot, unable to pull myself away, feeling stuck, yet knowing I wouldn't cross the road even if the opportunity to do so presented itself to me. As peculiar as my search for Flynn had become, being in North London looking for a church that didn't exist, and coming upon Julia's parents' house and peering at it for no reason, seemed even more puzzling.

Eventually, I found myself at the end of Blackwell Road again, on the high street. I crossed over and turned right again, trying to find a bus that would take me back to the West End. I decided to take the first left onto Leland Avenue, as I felt anxious and wanted to get home, hoping to find any bus stop along the way that might offer me a way out of the area. Halfway up Leland Avenue, I came upon a bus stop and hoped that if I waited there, salvation might appear in the form of a red double-decker bus.

I stood for the longest time, looking both ways, feeling confused and frustrated, struggling to understand how I ended up there—once again stuck in an unsettling situation, trying to find my way back home. Why had Emily sent me on this wild goose chase once again? None of it made any sense to me.

Leland Avenue's darkened landscape offered little in terms of any discernable light source. However, my attention became drawn to what appeared to be a small road or drive just across the avenue, with the faintest of light emanating from a small building tucked away on it. Once across the avenue, I made my way down this hidden, unnamed road and discovered a small church—St. Joseph's—which was nestled in amongst some rather tall trees. This had to be the church Emily referred to, however the building appeared closed, with only a dull light shining through a small window.

Still, there was an odd sense of familiarity about it. This street, with all its trees, reminded me of an area in Ravenswood, close to our family home, and this church's quaint architecture was like the Catholic church we belonged to. It all felt so strange. Even the parking area adjacent to the church, which was somewhat obscured by a smaller bank of trees, had that familiar feel to it. How odd all of it felt, and as my curiosity drew me further towards the church, I was suddenly startled by the voice of a man somewhere close behind me.

"Good evening."

As I turned, I discovered a man of the cloth, a priest I assumed, staring at me, and holding what looked like a bag of shopping. He appeared to be in his fifties, and as he drew nearer to me, I felt as though I recognized him, even though he was a stranger to me. I was taken aback and then realized I must have looked like a stalker, staring in at someone's property.

I did my best to offer a brief explanation.

"Hello. I'm sorry, I think I'm a bit confused. I was invited to a meeting at St. Joseph's, but I was told it was over on Riffington Road. I know this area, but I didn't know there was a church here."

The priest looked at me, perhaps sensing my desperation and confusion. He had a nice smile and when he finally spoke, he exuded a calm nature.

"Well, I didn't misinterpret your interest, so no need to worry. Hello, I'm Father John Appleton."

"So, this is your church?"

"Yes. It's rather modest, I know—probably why you never noticed it before. But I'm sorry, there's no meeting here this evening, and there's no church on Riffington Road."

Father Appleton seemed to eye me up and just maybe saw through the dark camouflage that was intended to hide me from view.

"Please come in, and once I've put my shopping away I can double-check to see if there were any meetings earlier, or maybe tomorrow. Our admin person may have scheduled something, as we do have a small conference room that community members can reserve for meetings and such. However, there's always a staff member present in the church, and I can assure you, there was no meeting here this evening."

We entered through a door into a small kitchen, where Father Appleton deposited his groceries accordingly. Once he organized himself, he invited me into the church.

"Have a look around. It's not a big place, but it suits our congregation."

After the brief tour, we headed back into the kitchen where he invited me to sit with him at a small table.

"I'm just going to look through our planner to see if there were any meetings yesterday, or scheduled for tomorrow. Can I make you a coffee or tea?"

Father Appleton had a kind face, and he looked over at me with a curious gaze as he thumbed through his planner. I declined the offer of a hot drink, and waited patiently to see if his search yielded anything helpful.

"So, do you know who would have reserved the room?"

"Well, I don't know. My friend Flynn Warner was apparently meeting with some people from a place called Studio K, but that's all I know."

Father Appleton looked across at me with a puzzled look on his face.

"Hmmm, well, I don't see anything down here. What was the meeting about?"

"I'm sorry, Father, I don't know. I think maybe about a community art project or something. I'm sorry for sounding so vague, but I was invited rather last minute and know very little about it—I'm starting to think I was given the wrong directions."

Father Appleton seemed genuinely concerned that I was unable to find my way.

"Oh dear, I wish I could've been more help to you."

"It's okay, Father, I guess it'll have to remain a mystery—at least until I track my friend down."

"Well, we all lose our way at times."

"I'm sorry, Father…you seem familiar to me, but I can't place where I might have seen you."

"Well, I've been around, and I've met a lot of people in my day, but I can't say I recognize you. Are you a religious person?"

"Umm, well, I'm Catholic, but haven't been to church for a while. I mean I still pray, but it's more of a solitary experience for me. I still have my faith and all, but yeah, my life took some unexpected turns some time ago, and things changed for me."

"Yes, I understand. But, as you said, you still have your faith and that's a good thing. You're American I assume—from the accent?"

"Yeah, I lived in England when I was young and moved back here after college."

"Odd how things work out for us. I've lived here and there, and then ended up being posted back close to where I came from."

I thanked Father Appleton for his help and told him I needed to be on my way. He looked at me again with concern in his eyes.

"I'm sorry you couldn't find your friend here. I hope you solve the mystery."

There was a feeling of warmth and comfort that swept over me as we spoke. I felt safe, tucked away inside that small kitchen, not wanting to leave and face the endless, looping search that was consuming my life. I felt grateful for the short respite, hidden in that small but secure sanctuary, and wanted to tell Father Appleton, but I knew those moments of respite were only brief and I had to face what awaited me outside the church doors.

We stood and faced each other, and shook hands. I thanked him again for taking the time to help me with my search. Father Appleton was quick to respond.

"No problem at all. Good luck and keep the faith."

I headed over to the door to leave, but before I made it over, Father Appleton offered me one last farewell.

"Have a good evening, Michael. I know it's dark out there tonight, so be careful on your way home."

His voice sounded familiar to me, and I stood frozen for a moment before turning back to him.

"That's odd, Father—I don't remember telling you my name. As a matter of fact, I don't remember introducing myself at all. How do you know my name?"

"I'm sure you told me—you may not have remembered doing so."

"It's strange; I just don't remember telling you my name."

He scratched his head and smiled.

"Well then, I guess we'll just have to consider that one a mystery as well. Oh, before you leave, I'd like to share something with you if you don't mind?" I nodded for him to continue. "Please listen, Michael. It's time now to look inward and forgive yourself."

His comment was both puzzling and unsettling.

"I don't understand, Father. What do you mean? About not attending church? Well, I stopped and all because of where things were in my life. That's it, nothing more."

"No, it's not about that, Michael. It's about you and this journey you've been on for such a long time. Most people, including myself, have had or will have similar life journeys, not all that different from your own in many respects. No matter what one believes—whether we were created by God or a supreme being of one's choosing, or whether we just came to be—we weren't made to be perfect. So, please forgive yourself, let go of what's holding you back, and get on with living."

As I continued to face Father Appleton, I heard a loud banging sound behind me, as if something had suddenly fallen over. I quickly swung around to look behind me, and without warning was overcome by a deep sense of fear. As I turned back to where Father Appleton had been standing, I was unexpectedly confronted by something so unexplainable and mystifying—yet at the same time, so comforting.

For now, standing in front of me was Sophie, my beautiful companion who reached out to me and guided me through a very puzzling landscape. I remembered this moment, this image of her, all belief suspended. She smiled at me as she had done so many times before, as we wandered through Nice, trying to solve the riddle of my missing friend. How could I make sense of such a moment? But there she stood, wearing the clothes I remember from my time with her in Nice.

"Sophie, what are you doing here? Where did Father Appleton go?"

Sophie walked over to me and grabbed my hands. Her smile and reassuring tone of voice brought a feeling of calm into the room, helping to expel the chaos that had followed me throughout this search for Flynn.

"Mike, I'm not sure who Father Appleton is. I'm just glad we had this opportunity to come together again."

I stood in disbelief, trying to make sense of how Sophie came to be here.

"I don't understand. This is a church, it's Father Appleton's church. You were in Nice. How did you know to come here? Did Flynn arrange this? Hold on, this is Flynn's doing, dragging me all over the place, isn't it?"

However, the compassionate look on Sophie's face told me otherwise—she understood my plight, knowing this search for Flynn had offered no resolve or respite. As she spoke, I remember listening closely to her words, to see if they would provide me with some sense of solace, some escape from this senseless path in life that had led me so far astray.

"Mike, I understand the sense of desperation you've felt. I also understand the pain you've experienced."

I was again puzzled.

"I don't get it. I mean, yeah, this search for Flynn has been exasperating at best."

Before I could speak further, Sophie had yet more to say.

"The desperation, the pain I speak of, is not about the search for Flynn. There's so much more to it. Wouldn't you agree?"

"What? I don't understand. I don't even know what you're trying to say to me. Why are you here in London? How did you find me in this place?"

"I've been here all along. Please listen to me. Everything will be fine."

I remember wanting to leave that room, desperate to go and take Sophie with me.

"Sophie, please come with me. I don't want to be alone with this anymore. I'm tired and lost…"

Sophie's expression of compassion remained. "I can't go with you right now. But listen—when you find your way back, I'll be waiting, and we'll be together again. It's time to stop meandering about. You've been on this journey of yours way too long. There's nothing else I can say right now that will help you understand. Time to find your way out. One last thing, and it's important—look for the light. It's out there, amongst all the darkness of your life."

As I held Sophie's hands in mine, I felt at a loss to understand what I had experienced since searching for Flynn. I desperately wanted her to come with me, but then suddenly and without warning, the door entering the kitchen from the outside suddenly blew open, banging loudly against the far wall. It startled me and I swung around to look, seeing only the dark of the night beyond the threshold of the door. As I turned back to Sophie, she had vanished, and I was no longer holding those reassuring hands in mine. All hope of understanding had left me, and it now seemed that my search for my lost friend was not to be solved—and worse, the circumstances of the search had now properly entered the realm of the bizarre.

I stood motionless for some time, focusing on the dull, yellowish glow from the ceiling light above, knowing there was only one path left for me to follow—across the waiting threshold and out into the darkness of the night.

I was without options, without any answers as to how to seek a way out of a tangled and muddled life that had kept me isolated and alone for so very long.

I made my way to the door and stepped out into an enigmatic world, one I no longer recognized or understood. It was so dark outside, and I stood for a moment undecided how to leave this area and make my way back home. But then it happened—a complete sense of disorientation swept over me, and this street, this area, it all became unrecognizable. This was not the part of North London that I had come to. I quickly turned back and remembered seeing the outlines of houses. St. Joseph's had disappeared as well, somehow obscured by the darkened void.

Panic had set in, and I began walking with a sense of urgency. I was in unknown territory, desperate and anxious, trying to calm my thoughts and wanting to make sense of what was happening to me. The disorientation and darkness only caused a deeper sense of panic. The street I walked along had houses on both sides, but no light emanated from any of them, as if they were lifeless, darkened cutouts, cast against a dispiriting backdrop. There were no streetlights, and I walked on not knowing where I was, or where I was headed. I was lost and alone, and without any idea how to escape this darkened maze.

Suddenly, amidst all the darkness, and in the distance, I could see a light, a bright light shining outward from a building—a house, I assumed. I walked towards it, but the anticipation of reaching the light got the better of me and I started to run, desperate to escape the darkness. My pace quickened, and then I sprinted, running towards the light, using up what reserves remained inside of my weary soul.

When I finally reached the light source, it was not a house, but what appeared to be a storefront of some kind. The light coming from inside radiated outward through a large glass window. It was so bright, I couldn't see anything inside—just light. I felt safe once again and wanted to stay there, and found myself facing the window, my hands pressed against the glass. I stared into the light, trying desperately to understand what was happening to me. I slowly slid to my knees, and I could feel my eyes closing, surrendering to the relentless fatigue that had plagued me throughout my search for Flynn.

When I opened my eyes once again and stared in, I saw images of my search from Nice, Paris, Michigan—the places I had visited and the people I met along the way. I saw Sophie again, and heard her voice and laughter, as she held in her arms the yellow and pink snapdragons. And despite my confusion, Sophie had come to me once again and I was kindly greeted by her beautiful brown eyes and her warm, charming smile.

I kneeled and placed my forehead against the large window, and there was the light, the illumination—for a brief instance, I was safe again. I felt warmth, and amidst my deep sense of confusion, I finally succumbed fully to the fatigue and to the best I can recall, I closed my eyes, and drifted between a sense of sleep and an odd panorama of images and fleeting sounds.

This mystical experience that for so long had led me astray, slowly began to fade away, and then, it was simply no longer.

CROSSING THOSE RICKETY BRIDGES

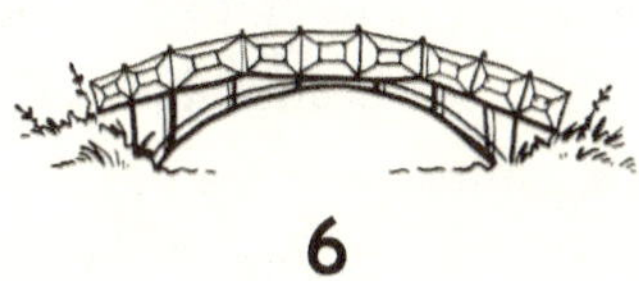

6

My eyes opened, slowly, and an abundance of light illuminated my surroundings. I was reclined, lying on my back, with medical equipment nearby. Upon awakening further, a rush of anxiety took hold, as the uncertainty of my situation left me disoriented. I felt tired, yet I struggled to wake, and my eyes again focused on the welcoming light.

As my level of consciousness increased, I remembered what had transpired to bring me to this hospital bed, in London's King's College Hospital. An errant bike rider had crashed into me at the bottom of my road, knocking me to the ground. Later, I would be told by the doctors and my mother that the violent collision had led me to hit my head against the pavement, as well as injuring the right side of my abdomen.

The doctors who attended to me, along with a consultant neurologist, explained that I experienced an unconscious period, followed by a wakeful and responsive state. I lay in a hospital bed for nearly two days, which confused me as I had no sense of time or how long I had been hospitalized. It was now late evening the following day. It was explained to me that I had been administered some rather strong drugs due to the extent of my injuries, and this contributed to my overall confused state and rather long slumber. I can remember having some tests and a scan done, and then being moved to the hospital room, but had little memory of anything afterward.

However, my longer-term memory appeared intact, and as I finally began to reawaken, details of my bewildering dream began to emerge, particularly of one beautiful young woman.

Janie, the attending nurse, was the unfortunate victim of my 'dream rant' as I rambled on, attempting to uncover some kernel of information that might help me understand—but I couldn't recall the identity of this mysterious woman. I explained how this dream was like choppy segments of different events woven together into one long, chronological narrative. I wanted someone to know and help me understand, but Janie simply told me it was probably the result of the accident trauma and heavy medication that was administered to help manage the pain. Yet I kept trying to make her understand that this incredibly vivid character in my dream was a mystery to me now—leaving me with nothing more than a puzzling, unforgettable image.

Janie tried her best to offer me reassurance by sticking closely to a redundant script.

"Look, you were very fortunate—some bruising on your right side, a couple of black eyes, and a few other scrapes, but the doctors said you were lucky there was no significant head injury. So just be patient with it all."

As it happened, my mother and sister Robyn—along with Robyn's two children, Richy, age seven and Chloe, age five—had come to England for a visit. I had made all the necessary arrangements for the time off and was looking forward to their trip. They arrived on Saturday, and being mid-June, it was summer break for the kids. My brother-in-law Peter remained in Chicago because of work commitments. I hadn't seen my mother or Robyn and her family for over a year, so it was to be a family reunion of sorts.

On the third afternoon of their visit, I made my way on foot to my local supermarket to buy a few things for the evening meal. On my way to the store, I walked a similar route as I often did, down to Rider's Grocers, a couple of blocks down from where I lived. As I approached the crossroads at the bottom of my own road, and as fate dictated on that day, a man on a pedal bike—Joshua Denton by name—was in a hurry to meet some friends, and thus our paths crossed.

Joshua, a thirty-five-year-old accountant—information passed on to me by my mother—had glanced down at his phone and mounted the sidewalk as the road was busy with traffic, when I stepped out from behind a hedge that ran along my road. He reported to the police and ambulance crew that he saw me too late and crashed into me, sending me to the pavement. It was reported that Joshua was clearly alarmed, and along with some good Samaritans who were passing by, attempted to support me as best they could before the ambulance crew arrived.

Upon my arrival at the hospital, the ambulance crew reported that I had been knocked unconscious by the fall, and that I was in a semi-conscious state on my way to the hospital. The head injury had been closely monitored, and Dr. John Gates—the neurologist who eventually met with me—simply said, "It was a very lucky escape."

However, despite all the reassurances, I still struggled to understand how I had little or no memory of lying in a hospital bed for all that time. More puzzling was how my mind could conjure up such a vivid memory of a woman during a reported dream state, yet in my conscious world, she simply remained an unknown. Dr. Gates felt that this mystery sighting was nothing more than a face in a dream, yet despite his rather pragmatic explanation, this enigmatic scenario left me wanting answers as to the identity of the beautiful visitor who guided me through the dark, challenging dreamscape. It made sense what Dr. Gates had said, yet it remained a mystery to me—all I knew for certain was that I had experienced one of the most incredible adventures of the mind that one could ever imagine. Dr. Gates did say that in terms of memory, there are occasions when events close to the injury or the event itself may result in an inability to recall details. These memories can return at some point, however each case is different.

I was given further assurance that there appeared to be no significant issues linked to memory loss. Yet I felt unsure of it all, and despite memories of the accident and subsequent events being somewhat intact, why was it that there was this memory, this face, this voice, this alluring accent, and this beautiful image of a woman that I simply could not remember? Despite my efforts to impress upon anybody, including my mother and sister, how vivid this dream had been in my mind, there was no way to convince anyone of the experience that had transpired while I lay in that hospital bed. As requested, my mother had brought me a pen and paper, as I wanted to ensure that no detail of this unsettling dream was forgotten. I would write it all down, every moment, in as much detail as I could recall.

Much to my disappointment, I was forced to stay one more night in the hospital, mainly for observation purposes. Before leaving the hospital the next day, I was given exhaustive paperwork to read, including precautionary measures and things to avoid over the next week or so. I was managing okay, despite a fair amount of pain, a bit of irritability and still feeling rather unsettled.

Oddly enough, for some time, I had pondered the idea of looking up a mental health counselor for the purpose of exploring potential issues around my career uncertainty and feelings of isolation I had been wrestling with over the last few years. Fortuitously contained within the paperwork was a leaflet on counseling services. In the company of my mother and sister, I queried the doctor who was reviewing the discharge information as to how the referral process would work. He offered to circumnavigate the process by having the hospital make the referral for me, and as a result I would be short-listed and seen in a timelier manner. It was a quick decision on my part, and with positive affirmations from both my mother and sister, I gave him the go-ahead.

I was still quite sore because of the accident, but felt fortunate I hadn't sustained significant injury. I collected my paperwork and along with my family, made my way along the hospital corridors to the front entrance. My hospital experience had come to an end, and I was anxious to get home.

My two-night stay in the hospital had left me with much to ponder, and my restless mind once again came alive with an array of thoughts and lingering images from my otherworldly sleep experience.

As we left the hospital, my mother was already insisting that she would be staying on for a few more days "to make sure everything was okay."

Despite my resistance and assurances, she remained determined until I told her I wanted to return to my usual routine as soon as possible, and that lengthening her stay would not be necessary. I had missed my mother since moving back to England. She was an incredible woman, full of energy and optimism, always living up to her nickname, 'Zippy'—one that had been given to her many years ago by her parents, a reference to her constant state of motion.

It felt a bit strange walking out of the hospital into the London landscape, but I was glad to be going home. I loved the summer months, and it was bright out, sunny, and warm, a perfect late afternoon in the city. Once inside the black cab, the ride home to Greenwich felt reassuring to me, and as we made small talk traveling through the London streets, I slowly began to feel a budding reconnection to both my mother and sister.

Shortly after walking through the door of my apartment, my mother quickly began preparations for the evening meal. She made us all a hot drink and insisted we sit and talk for a while. I felt a sense of relief sweep over me. It was an oddly emotional return, and I fought back tears as I watched my mother scurry about, ensuring my homecoming was to be as comfortable as possible.

We didn't talk much about the accident, all of us realizing that for now, it had been talked out. My mom did tell me that Joshua Denton had phoned the hospital and spoken to her. She said he was struggling with what had happened, and asked if I could contact him when the time was right. I made a note to phone him, as I felt it was important to offer him some reassurance that all was well.

Our conversation eventually swung over to my 'mystical journey' as Robyn had now titled my hospital dream experience. The one thing that seemed to intrigue my mother was how this elusive woman had become a part of this wild narrative.

"Interesting," she said, "that you'd have such a strong image of this woman. A woman with a French accent, so clearly burned into your memory. I believe she's out there, somewhere."

Fantastic, a mother's optimism.

"Am I too preoccupied with this? I mean, am I focusing too much on this whole thing? I just don't know. This dream was so surreal, and this woman was such a big part of it all."

My mom, forever the optimist, was eager to step in.

"Michael, I think you'll remember her one day. I understand how important it is to you, and yes, it makes sense that she occupies a place in your head. Just don't become obsessive. Let it come, and just maybe it will all be revealed to you as the doctor said."

It all made sense what she was saying, though less easy to put into practice. The problem was only a first name and a face left very little for me to start my research. I did think that, just maybe, something would trigger my memory and I would solve this mystery before too long, but that might be wishful thinking.

Only time would tell.

THAT EVENING, THE THREE of us sat and talked about my feeling disconnected from my family. In the course of this conversation, I wanted to acknowledge my mother's devotion to me over the years, despite my rather irrational behavior. How could one create an inventory of what a dedicated and loving mother does for her children throughout their lives? I felt an incredible debt of gratitude towards her, and as I sat trying to explain myself, I wanted this dear woman to know that the love I felt for her had never diminished.

My situation with Robyn, however, had been different. I found reasons to cut myself off from her after my father died—despite her best efforts to keep the lines of communication wide open. Because of the unyielding and relentless commitment she had made to both my mother and father over the years, never saying no to any opportunity to share precious life moments with them, she herself had become a painful reminder to me of my unwillingness to maintain and value those very same precious opportunities—opting instead to indulge myself in whatever nonsensical distraction or self-indulgence gave me reason to stay away.

Yet, Robyn never gave up, writing me emails, phoning, sending me photos of the kids and family events. It was all so unfortunate, and sadly, this brilliant older sister who held on despite my best intentions to break away, was forced to stand back and witness my withdrawal from a distance. How ironic, considering she always remained an incredible role model throughout my life. So, I continued to live with a deep sense of guilt for ignoring Robyn after I moved to England—how does one make up for all that lost time and the damage done?

So goes the story of my sister Robyn, and our relationship. In many respects, she was probably the most loyal individual I had ever known. A supportive wife, a loving mother, a precious daughter, and my beautiful older sister. She was an incredible sibling to me throughout my younger years—tolerant, caring, and despite what she described as my obnoxious tendencies when we were growing up, she always made time for me. In many ways, Robyn understood my struggles when we relocated to England better than anyone. She would often meet me after school and would always talk to me about how I was feeling being so far away from our homeland.

When motherhood eventually came along, Robyn quickly shifted gears and found herself having to balance family responsibilities and a part-time career. However, through it all, and much like my mother, her duty and loyalty to family remained her top priority— hence her ongoing persistence in keeping a wayward brother within her loving reach.

I tried, rather awkwardly, to explain how life had changed for me after my father had died. Yet it became clear to me that the disconnect with both my mother and Robyn lay solely at my feet. The gaps between our visits had been too long, and because I clearly made a determined effort at times to not return phone calls or respond to emails, claiming I was too busy to speak with them, an unfortunate distance had resulted. In part, by closing the communication channels, I could avoid those uncomfortable discussions and questions that would sadly resurrect past times that I had chosen to hide from. Ironically, in the end, my misaligned attempt to justify my wayward mindset contributed to an ever-widening gap between us, and did little to diminish the memories that remained in relentless pursuit of me. Yet, in some peculiar way, I had convinced myself that I had not disconnected from them, that it was down to my chaotically busy London life. However, looking back, how could this be? It could be described as an emotional paradox of sorts, an admission of guilt and self-blame on one hand, and a very odd sense of denial on the other. This was the battle inside my head that clearly continued to live on, without me truly understanding why.

After my rather clumsy attempts to apologize, my mother took the lead and was honest in her appraisal of my past behavior. Her approach to me was considerate, yet honest.

"I know things have been difficult for you, but please, let's make sure this doesn't happen again. We're a small family—so let's keep and value what we have."

In saying this, she spared me from experiencing yet more shame for my past actions. There had been no lack of effort on their part to reach out over the last few years, yet it was my resistance and confusion that led to my self-imposed state of exile, apart from the two people who cared for me the most.

At some point my mother raised a subject that clearly both she and Robyn had wanted to discuss with me. They were surprised at my willingness to engage with a professional therapist. Oddly, my explanation was quite straightforward, and clearly linked to the gap that had formed between us. When my father died, I thought I managed this major life event with a sense of maturity and acceptance, and as a result quashed any outward grief that so often seemed to plague others when confronted with such difficult situations. I continued to insist to everyone that I had it all figured out. I truly believed that I had moved on, and made life choices that were in my best interest. I put feelings of grief aside, believing

I was one of the few who could survive such a tragic event without any apparent emotional scarring. It was something that I prided myself on, because I'd supposedly weathered the storm in such a capable manner.

When I moved back to England to work for North Star Media, I was commended by my superiors for bringing an impressive sense of professionalism to the job. It was all good—or at least I thought it was. But as life moved on in England, I was beginning to discover that I was quite alone, and distant from those around me. I was always a bit of a loner, particularly as a child, so none of this felt particularly out of place. I could always manage to say the right things, or act like all was okay, but it soon became apparent that I was slowly cutting myself off from mainstream life, from those people who cared for me. I found my life became all a hollow routine, and though I was safe and comfortable within my own little space, I was isolated and apart from the world outside.

I began to recognize that I had retreated from life, and that such reliance on routine was not a healthy option. Because of my life choices, I began to be plagued by self-doubt, and my self-esteem began to erode. I felt angry with myself and others for no apparent reason. I once believed that much of that lack of confidence from my younger years had left me as I matured into a young man, but after my father's death, it became clear that it hadn't.

And then, without warning, all that anger and fear and self-doubt had stealthily crept into my life and set me even further apart from the world around me. Still, I didn't know. I wasn't an expert in psychology or mental health, so I couldn't understand what was happening. What I did know was that my life had become oddly unsettling, in spite of its ostensible comfort and safety.

Because of this confusion, I began to question why it was I continued to accept this life of emotional stagnation, and what it was that kept me so fastened to this safe place, inaccessible to the life that surrounded me. So, I did some research on the therapeutic process, hoping that I might gain some insight as to how it might support me, or at the very least offer me the opportunity to hear what an objective voice might tell me. I did, however, wonder if it would help at all.

This debate continued within me for some time, before I decided that hearing what an objective voice might have to say may not be such a bad thing after all. With that, my mind was made up.

But it never happened. I procrastinated, and convinced myself that waiting for the right time to begin the process was the right thing to do—and, as so often goes, the plans fell by the wayside. However, when the leaflet appeared in the discharge paperwork at the hospital, I truly believed I was meant to receive it. Why not go for it? So, my decision was quick, and giving the nod of approval for a fast-track referral seemed like a logical choice.

Before we retired for the evening, Robyn raised the topic of my dream state while in the hospital. I found myself eager to share more details of it with the two of them, hoping for some clarity or understanding as to what it all meant. We went over some of the notes I had written down, but never in our conversations did either of them ever recall me speaking of a woman named Sophie. Robyn teased me that, from my description, Sophie sounded rather exotic and maybe she was a girl of many a man's dream. I guess it didn't help hearing that, even if Robyn was right. But why the face, the voice, the touch? I could only believe I knew this woman from somewhere. I guess I held out hope that Sophie would come walking through the door at any minute, with her beautiful face, dressed in her lovely clothes that I remembered from my dream, with her bright smile lighting up everything around her.

But I had to focus on the reality of it all—at this point Sophie was only a face in a dream, much like Dr. Gates had told me in the hospital. But Robyn's persistence in asking questions about my hospital experience reminded me, that despite my desire to understand all that had transpired during this puzzling dream narrative, maybe the answers to those questions would never be forthcoming. However, inside I knew, this was something I needed to explore. There was already something there, pushing me to get this search going, to find the answers to those tough questions and to discover the identity of this mystery woman whose image and memory had found its way into the forefront of my mind.

We decided to call it a night. I was tired and was looking forward to sleeping in my own bed. When we finally said goodnight, I felt a huge sense of relief, and thought what a powerful force love and connection is in a person's life. In the end, despite my past attempts at separating myself from my mother and sister, they never gave up on me, and persisted in the belief, that when the time was right, I would return to them.

FLYNN AND EMILY CAME over the next evening, rambling across Blackheath Common in a light but steady rain. They had arrived for dinner, a celebration of sorts orchestrated by my mother and sister. Upon entering, the two were greeted with hugs and kisses, with much attention being given to Emily and her growing bump. My facial injuries took them by surprise, and both expressed how upset they were when they received the call from my mother.

It had been some time since my mother and Robyn had laid eyes on Flynn, and everyone was anxious to have a long-overdue catch-up. Flynn was ecstatic to see both my mother and Robyn and the kids, and after a brief re-cap of my accident and hospital adventure, they both fired questions at me about how I was feeling.

I assured them that, some cautionary measures aside, I would be back to my normal routine as soon as possible.

As the conversation meandered, Flynn took charge and was curious to hear about life back in Chicago, and how things were going with my family. The kids were eager to chime in too, and Flynn and Emily enjoyed hearing all about the family adventures. As I sat back and listened to them all talk about times past and what had transpired over recent years, I was struck by the fact that connections are never really lost, and still can be valued even though we may lead separate lives. As I sat and listened, I smiled at it all and felt a sense of togetherness I had not experienced for a very long time. I missed these times as I hid away from it, feeling that maybe I didn't deserve to feel good about life or even have the pleasure of sharing in the lives of friends and family. I didn't understand it all, but I wanted to experience those feelings again, to laugh out loud and participate in the celebration of living.

After a brilliant dinner, Flynn and Emily were anxious to hear about my dream. I sat back and took my time, proceeding to tell Flynn and Emily everything. Both were intrigued by what I had described as Flynn's missing person status. We even had a laugh about it, and Flynn promised me he had no intention of leaving his lovely wife, ever. Emily stared in disbelief at times, fascinated as my mom and Robyn had been about my dream.

I was meticulous in detailing the mystery girl who made her way into my life via my dream state, and the circumstances in which she appeared. I described her appearance down to every last facial freckle—as I had with my mother and Robyn—and highlighted my conversations with this beguiling woman who spoke with the most beautiful French accent. I felt hopeful that, just maybe, Flynn knew this beautiful woman from a conversation we may have had in the past.

Flynn looked at me for the first time with a blank expression. He quickly exchanged glances with Emily, who had an equally blank look on her face.

"I don't know any Sophie," Flynn said, a little sadly. "I'm trying hard to think if maybe we met her when we all went to France together, but no, I just can't remember."

What proved more disheartening was that, despite neither he nor Emily having any recollection of Sophie, they also couldn't recall me ever speaking of anyone by that name. It didn't make sense to me. I struggled to understand why this incredible person would have imprinted herself on my mind, and yet those people who knew me best could not even remember me speaking of her. But they promised to think on it together and see if maybe they had some recollection of who she might be, or if we all met somewhere in France. They both tried to maintain an optimistic frame of mind about it all, but there was nothing familiar about my dream girl they could remember.

Flynn was anxious to change the subject and talk about a cooperative effort between my magazine and an innovative art center that was being developed in Paris. As it stood, Flynn's friends Samuel and Estelle—both lifelong Parisians, artists, and art teachers—had created a community scheme to bring art to those who'd never had access or opportunity to enjoy it before, starting at a grassroots level. A consortium of fellow artists and friends, along with two city-wide grants, had allowed them to purchase a disused two-story building to begin this incredible project of bringing art to the people. There were to be classes, discussion groups, family art projects, artist lectures, and more. There were even plans to broaden the scope by integrating photography, videography, and film study into the project.

After some initial discussion between myself and the development team driving the art project, Flynn and I presented the idea to my editor, Jon Finney, who gave the go-ahead for me to do a full-length article on the development of this project. Flynn's face lit up when we discussed it. He and I had previously sat down and drawn up a timetable for our visits to Paris. I wanted to ensure that, before we made our way over, the project was up and running so we could highlight the workings of the center and focus on the participants and community members who were partaking in the various courses offered through the scheme.

Flynn said there was no fixed date as to when we were to head over to France, though late August had been mooted as a possible first visit. The project was still in the early stages, but was up and running, so we had plenty of time to discuss dates, allowing me time to hopefully learn some remedial French. Flynn encouraged this as he thought it might be helpful during our trips to Paris, even though I'd certainly need his support and his fluency to assist me.

Before the two of them said their goodbyes, we agreed to meet up after my family had returned to America.

"We can discuss our Paris arrangements," Flynn said with a real sense of anticipation. "It's gonna be a lot of fun."

With that, Flynn and Emily bid farewell to my family, and made a promise to send photos of the baby once they made their way into the world. As Flynn and Emily made their way out, I was grateful to be a part of such a warm gathering, and was appreciative that, at the very least, there were caring people in my life who would not let me fade into obscurity.

LATE MORNING THE NEXT day, Jon Finney came by to see me. My role as a feature writer at *Narrator* magazine was due in no small part to Jon's support. I was most fortunate to meet Jon when he paid a visit to the North Star Media offices in Chicago. North

Star, who owned *Narrator* and other UK-based magazines and publications, arranged a meeting between Jon and myself, as I had previously expressed an interest in returning to London and working on North Star's UK-based publications. After a series of interviews and subsequent discussions, I was offered the opportunity to join his team.

Narrator magazine was the brainchild of North Star and Jon Finney, and after some research on my part, I found the role of feature writer for a human-interest-based publication to be the perfect fit. The magazine had a simple but appealing ethos—sharing the stories of real people and celebrating their aspirations, achievements, or simply their place in life. In short, it was about the human experience, and it didn't matter where the stories came from. London and UK life became the targeted focus area of the magazine, but an occasional 'out-of-area feature' was always appreciated, hence the stamp of approval for my Paris art house project. Jon didn't care where the stories came from, as long as there was a meaningful story to be told.

Jon spent a bit of time chatting with my mother and sister and her kids, before they made their way out the door and down to Greenwich Park.

As with Flynn and Emily, Jon was quick to ask me about the accident and shook his head with dismay at the circumstances and outcome of my encounter.

"Well, I must admit I was quite alarmed when I heard the news. It's good seeing you, even with all your bumps and bruises. I mean, what might have been—one dreads to think. I'm so glad you're okay."

After chatting for some time about the accident and my hospital stay, and discussing details about my return to work, Jon said his goodbyes and said he only wanted me back when I felt ready.

Before Jon left, I couldn't let him out the door without asking,

"Jon, do you remember me speaking about a woman by the name of Sophie?"

Jon looked at me with a puzzled look on his face.

"Who is she, Mike?"

"So, you don't know?"

"I don't know the name and I don't remember you talking about any woman. Should I know her?"

"You're positive it doesn't sound familiar?"

Jon stood motionless for a couple of moments, trying to recall anything.

"No, nothing that I can remember. So, who is she? Is it important?"

"I don't know. Just somebody I don't want to forget, is all. But oddly enough, I have to remember her first."

Jon looked at me and grabbed my hand.

"So glad you're okay. I'll let the team know how you're getting on."

Maybe taking a few extra days off wasn't such a bad thing. I was certain of one thing however—my investigation into discovering the identity of my mystery woman had now become a priority, and I was determined to find her, no matter how long or how much effort it would require.

After Jon left, I sat for a while and scanned the internet about head injuries, comas, concussions, and such. Head trauma was nothing to take lightly, and I felt most fortunate to have escaped this incident with, I hoped, no long-term impact. It was unsettling to think what might have happened, as Jon had stated. In an instant, a person's life could change in such a dramatic fashion.

I did manage to scan through two medical articles on amnesia, which highlighted retrograde and anterograde amnesia. I decided it was best not to discuss my fears or concerns with others, but I was perplexed as to why I could not recall this woman who appeared in my dream state. I was already concerned about my obsession with the whole thing, but why couldn't I remember her? Had the fall impacted my memory more than the doctors had recognized?

What I learned through further reading was how complex the science around the brain and related trauma was, and how individuals could be impacted in life-changing ways. I scanned through information on the minimally conscious state, post-concussion syndrome and other rather complex states linked to brain trauma. Retrograde amnesia, as explained to me in the hospital, was when 'one cannot recall memories that were formed before the event.' Dr. Gates indicated that in some cases, memories just before an event may be lost—however he did not believe I had experienced any significant loss of memory. He assured me that the dream state was nothing more than that, and that the woman I remembered from the dream was probably something my mind created. Still, when I awoke in that hospital bed the next day, why did I feel such profound confusion and disorientation, my mind cluttered with images and dialogue from a long and winding collection of stopping points as I attempted to find my way back home? There was so much to it, and so much I didn't understand.

I even scanned a few articles about individuals who experienced dream states when in a coma. But I wasn't in a coma—I simply slept in a hospital bed after being given some pain medication. That was it—at least, that's what was told to me. I attempted to clear my mind and put my anxieties aside before my family returned from the park. I had to find some sense of separation between myself and this intrusive obsession with trying to remember who the face and lovely French accent belonged to—even though she may not actually exist.

I felt okay physically. The bruising was sore and uncomfortable at times, but I suffered no lasting physical repercussions and was so grateful for that. It was unsettling to think what could have been, but I was upright and hopefully thinking clearly once again, and anxious to get on with life.

THE TIME WITH MY family had come to an end. I traveled with them to the airport, facing the reality of having to say goodbye. Despite my accident, we had a meaningful visit, and the opportunity to reconnect was something I needed in my life. Saying goodbye, especially after feeling that I had started to properly reconnect with both my mom and sister, was harder than I'd expected. It was my family, all that I had in this world, and the time we spent together was a promising beginning to restoring my relationships with them.

There was a clear hesitancy on my mother's part to leave, but I assured her that I needed to get on with life as well, and I promised to keep in touch every week. No more gaps in contact or making excuses to not speak. My mother was right to tell me that I had separated myself from them—so as a result, a renewed commitment and new priorities were required of me. Maybe the accident had oddly awakened me. It reminded me just how fragile life could be. I needed to return to my family, that much I knew—it was important that I did the work to bring them back into my life.

I wandered around the airport until their flight had departed, and afterward, as I stood alone in the airport, I experienced a moment of complete sadness. My eyes filled with tears, and I felt scared and alone, and wasn't sure at this very moment where my life might be heading. Still, I was grateful for this opportunity to begin to reclaim all that I had lost along the way.

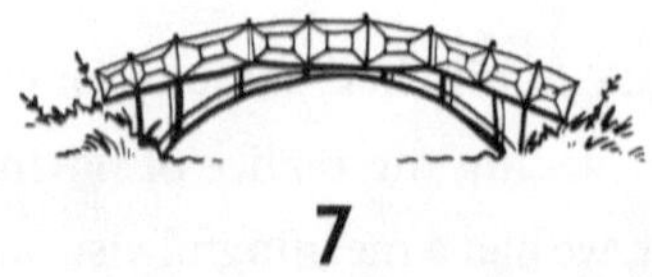

7

A letter had arrived at my flat shortly after the accident and stay in the hospital. An appointment had been made for me to meet with a therapist at the Green Gardens Centre near London Bridge. The center was part of a campus area, which included an array of professionals, including physical and occupational therapists, specialist doctors, mental health practitioners, and others. Many of these individuals were part of a network of private and public-based support services.

The appointment was just over two weeks from the day I left the hospital. I had little time to think it over, but despite some nerves, I knew I had to jump into it or risk never going at all. During the two-week period between my hospital stay and the scheduled appointment, I managed to review the very detailed journey of my dream narrative, which I had recorded in the journal my mother had given to me. I had also taken a couple extra days to rest up, but was anxious to get back to work, so upon my return I reviewed my deadlines and looming appointments and made an action plan, surprising myself at my ability to organize my work duties in such an efficient manner. I was eager to keep the wheels turning.

My appointment with Dr. Olivia Whitney at the Green Gardens Centre was suddenly upon me. It was certainly new territory for me, but I was not averse to it and accepted the notion that it would hopefully be a beneficial experience. I wasn't sure about any preparation, or if I should bring anything along with me, so all I brought was the journal filled with the narrative I had recorded from my hospital dream, plus a pen that consisted of two plastic halves, which came apart, exposing the simple metal filler. It was the perfect therapy tool, ideal for moments of stress when this most practical of fidget gadgets was available as needed. Whenever I was in a meeting, the pen traveled with me, occupying, or distracting me as the need dictated.

I felt ready for the appointment, and with my journal of notes in hand, I was prepared to start the process. I had even transcribed some notes from a digital recorder onto the pad, so no details about the dream would be lost.

I arrived at the facility quite early, and made my way through the building at a relaxed, leisurely pace. Dr. Olivia Whitney's office was on the third floor of the five-floor facility. The reception area was quiet and adorned with comfortable furniture, subtle colors, and had a relaxing ambiance.

After checking in with the reception staff, I waited patiently, feeling my anxiety growing. I had no strong feelings one way or the other. I promised myself to be cautious, and certainly possessed some skepticism about it all. Yet, I knew I had to give it a chance.

Eventually, Dr. Whitney made her way to the waiting area to greet me. She was not what I had expected. Early forties, long dark hair, and dressed more casually than I had imagined. She wore gray casual trousers, a black and gray blouse, and a colorful cardigan, buttoned once in the middle. She wore large-framed glasses, which made her look the part of a librarian—a rather attractive librarian at that. Once in her office however, the glasses came off.

"I need them for reading and computer work," she said by way of explanation, "so I normally don't wear these around too much."

She had a nice smile and a comfortable, cheery tone to her voice. I wasn't sure what I had expected, however first impressions were positive. Her office felt relaxing. The far window looked down on the courtyard, which sat in the middle of the well-manicured campus area. I made a comment on the office, so she gave me the briefest of tours. With several green plants scatted about, the environment had a comfortable feel to it.

The first order of business was introductions. She preferred Olivia and I opted for Mike. It was a good start. After some small talk, Olivia explained the process and focused on her counseling modality and style. She was a cognitive-behavioral therapist, and our collaborative objective would be exploring life experiences and events, and how decision-making is linked to emotions, behaviors, and patterns of thinking. All sounded good to me.

Olivia commended me for my willingness to engage in the process.

"Hopefully this experience will be meaningful to you. And in terms of how long you will be attending, that will be up to you. This is your time, your journey. We want this to work for you."

And so, the process began, as Olivia kicked things off.

"So, what would you like to talk about today?"

"Well, um, I hadn't really thought of it I guess." I attempted a smile but was careful not to appear awkward or helpless. "I'm not sure. I'm generally quite a private person, so I'm not accustomed to this kind of thing. I thought maybe you wanted me to talk about the accident I had?"

I felt a bit uncomfortable, but Olivia was quick to help me out.

"Well, I think at some point we can talk about the accident, but I don't see that as being a priority right now. If you could let me know what's going on with you right now, that would be great. If you don't want to continue, then that's fine. But let's give it a go for a bit, and just see how you feel about it all."

Olivia had a warm, reassuring smile. What she was saying made sense. I sat for a moment, not sure where to start. But she quickly stepped in once again.

"I see you brought a notebook with you."

So, despite my promise to be cautious, I thought why not start there? I had convinced myself that I had brought the notebook along to review my thoughts when waiting out in the reception area. But perhaps I wanted to share the details with her, if it felt right.

"Yeah, there's something that I've written down that may or may not be significant. But I guess I wouldn't be honest if I didn't tell you that I am experiencing a bit of restlessness and some anxiety in my life right now as well. So, I didn't want to leave that out, just in case you felt we should start there."

"Let's just see where it all goes. Emotions, thoughts, feelings you are experiencing—it's all good. Let's take it slow and I think we'll find our way. If you would indulge me, I'd like to hear about your notebook and what's in there, because you brought it and there must be something in there that you feel is important. Is that okay? Does that make sense?"

"It does. I guess I would like to share what this notebook is about." It felt like the honest thing to say. And I felt some relief at saying it.

Olivia settled back into her chair, and I began to explain in detail what I dreamt about, or experienced. As I quickly reviewed my hospital stay and the freakish dream I had there, I became aware that I was playing with my pen, something that Olivia ignored. I was careful to ensure that I didn't make a lot of noise with it—the challenge became to reassemble and assemble it in a manner that did not prove annoying or distracting. I did force myself on a couple of occasions to stop, and simply hold the small pen in my hand. I gave a precis of what I had experienced—my missing friend, the search, where the search led me, and how I simply didn't understand what it all meant, if anything. I even mentioned my father during my quick overview.

Olivia listened intently, only stopping me once to ask a question.

"How did you record all of this?"

"Well, I wrote it on this pad and made notes on my digital recorder. It was all quite interesting, because I didn't think the doctors quite understood how dramatic this dream was. I don't think I can make anybody understand it. It was so real, yet so surreal. It was one long narrative, one long story, and I'd never experienced anything like it before. I remembered everything in so much detail, all of it, including the order of events, and the images of course. It was like I lived it. There was so much detail—people, places, sounds, things I can't explain, and it was all connected like one long event."

I did describe my mystery woman, but didn't spend too much time focusing on her. I wanted it all to make sense to Olivia, to make her understand what I had experienced. She waited patiently before responding.

"Okay, I think it's going to be important that, during your next appointment, we begin to explore and discuss this—and maybe look at the narrative and what was going on with it all. I think there's value in digging deeper, because this narrative may have more significance than you realize—so let's give it some time. Is that okay?"

Olivia summarized what we had discussed. She then asked if I would be willing to share with her something from my life at the current time that has made me feel good. It didn't take long.

"Well, my mother and sister and my niece and nephew came to visit me from the States. It was nice to reconnect again, despite the accident. I've been a bit detached from them in recent years, so having them over was good. It was nice being together again.

I miss them a lot—much more than I realized, I guess. And I was fortunate that they were here when this accident happened."

Olivia offered a warm smile in response, before asking me a bit more about family. I spoke in more detail about my mom and Robyn, before we moved on.

Olivia then asked me what the rest of my day looked like, and she seemed pleased that despite returning to work, I was looking after my immediate needs. Before I left, she said it was important to phone her office if anything proved difficult in the interim. She did emphasize that she was confident this process would be helpful to me.

"Mike, thank you for coming here and I look forward to seeing you next week."

With that, my first session ended. I felt hopeful as I made my way out. Even though it was just a start, at least I had somebody impartial there to listen.

THE NEXT WEEK SEEMED to pass by without anything significant happening. My job occupied my time once again, and with some new assignments and subsequent deadlines in place, work life was back in full swing.

My next counseling appointment with Olivia came around quickly, and a sense of anticipation and purpose was in the air as I set off to my now-regular Thursday meeting. I was anxious to see her again, and eager to talk through my dream in more detail, as evidenced by the blue journal I carried in my hand.

We exchanged pleasantries and Olivia was curious to know how my past week had been. I shared what highlights there were, and told her I had been in a rather reflective state, thinking of times past—most likely brought on by my brief reunion with my mother and Robyn. Olivia listened intently, and then seemed eager to discuss my dream-state narrative, or as I described it, 'my unconscious wanderings.'

"I like that label. Bit of mystique about it all. So, like I said last week, a good place to start."

"I know it was just a dream, but it left such a strong impression, so I guess I just want to talk about it and make some sense of it all. I want to share it with someone who might have some insight into it. I just don't think others, including my mom and sister, could understand how this dream was so complex and surreal. I hope that makes sense."

Olivia listened carefully and then replied, "I can appreciate how that must feel to you, but it is your experience and others won't fully understand it, even me. I want to hear in detail what you have to say, so maybe we can begin to unravel it. You know, I consider myself to be a person of science in many respects. But I believe that there are things in life we can't always explain through science, or by being pragmatic in our approach all the time. I think this narrative deserves all the attention you want to give it. It may have more significance than you realize. So, let's go exploring and see where we end up."

So, I started again, and then it came to Sophie. I explained to Olivia that I had made a journey over to France with Flynn and Emily about three years ago, and that perhaps I had met her there. This mystery woman was clearly French, so that felt like a logical conclusion to draw, even if Flynn and Emily didn't remember her. I also explained that my internet search for Sophie hadn't yielded anything. What was interesting, I explained, was that I recognized everybody else throughout that entire narrative—even Madame Giron, whom I had only met briefly when we stayed in Nice.

"It just seems so odd that this young woman was so prominent in my narrative, yet I don't remember her."

"So, tell me more about Sophie," Olivia said, a curious expression on her face.

And so, I continued. Every detail, every aspect of her beautiful face, figure, hair, voice, even down to how she was dressed. It was so nice to unburden myself in this way, to share Sophie with someone else who really listened.

"I don't want you to think I'm obsessed. I mean, I'm not I don't think, but I just want to remember her. I know you don't necessarily want to give an opinion on it, but can you tell me what you think right now—I mean, do you think she is a real person, or did I make her up, an image of someone who is not real as the doctors suggested? I need to know if I'm just chasing my own tail here."

Olivia was patient and appeared in a thoughtful state before she answered.

"Well, I think it's early days. I think if we invest more time into this, we may figure a lot of this out. It's a hard question to answer. After listening to this narrative, and the role that this woman played in it—well, she stands out as a bit of everything that was nice, safe, warm, and loving. A lot of what happened in this narrative was unsettling, and it was filled with anxiety, fear, darkness, loss, frustration, grief, and you were caught in this unknown place without a way out. Yet, through this all, Sophie seemed like the one person or one element that kept you safe, or gave you a reason to move on, even telling you in the end how to find your way out. She was your translator, that safe place to go to. She was your light in all that darkness. It's a very powerful image."

I smiled at her.

"St. Francis' prayer. Somebody gave me a sympathy card when my father died with that line on the front."

Olivia looked me over before replying, "I think we all search for those things in life, answers to those mysteries that surround our lives, because humans are curious creatures, and in some ways we all seek answers each day of our lives—and when times are difficult or challenging, or dark, we often seek the light amongst it all. So, maybe she's real, maybe she's not."

I was impatient, however, and awkwardly asked Olivia outright, "So please help me here. I appreciate what you said, and it makes sense, but you must have an opinion. I won't be upset if it isn't what I want to hear, but I just want somebody to say yes or no."

Olivia smiled broadly.

"Well, I think the brain is an amazing thing, and is capable of so many things, even while we sleep. I think this image of this young woman became your guide and she gave you hope. There must be a reason for that."

I felt a bit downcast after hearing Olivia's response, and my frustration was heightened because of her vague response to my plea. Maybe I couldn't make her understand.

"If I've given it too much significance, if that's what's being said here, then I guess I have to accept that which I can't resolve."

It was clear Olivia could read the frustration on my face.

"All I'm saying is that I think it's in your best interest if we explore what else was happening in this dream, because we need to understand the nature of the search. Why did your mind create a construct of a missing friend? Maybe we need to understand what you were really searching for. Clearly, you weren't searching for your missing friend. Memories of your father were there, your ex-partner, distant relatives, even a Catholic priest and more—and you ran and ran in this dream, jogging without direction, often trying to find your way. You were caught in a loop. Why? Who is to say if Sophie is real or not? Maybe she was a nurse in the hospital, a stranger that sat next to you on the bus, or a woman you caught a glimpse of at your local coffee shop at some time in the past, or somebody you saw at the supermarket. Who knows? If we can figure out more of this puzzle, I think we might be able to figure out who Sophie is, and what she was doing there."

It was then that Olivia finally weighed in and gave me an answer to my very enigmatic query.

"I'm sorry for my evasiveness. You deserve an answer. So, I'm going to say yes, I believe she's a real person. I'm reluctant to say that to you, as I don't want to dangle false hope in front of you, because Sophie may prove to be elusive, and I think becoming too focused on her might lead us away from what we really need to explore. But yes, I believe she's real, more than likely somebody you've met—somebody you spent some time with. I don't believe this mystery woman would impact you in this way if you simply saw her in passing. I can't explain why you can't remember her, but like I said, if we can better understand what was happening around you when she was sheltering you, then perhaps all will be revealed."

I felt a sudden wave of emotion sweep over me. I didn't know what it was, exactly. Maybe relief, maybe sadness. I felt tears forming, and I felt embarrassed, so I did my best to hide it all, but Olivia saw through it.

"Listen, we aren't giving up on this investigation. We just need to broaden it a bit, is all."

Before I left, Olivia asked me to trust the process and gave assurances that, together, we would solve some of the mystery of the runaway narrative. Maybe not all of it, but there was a lot left to explore.

As I strolled through the London streets after leaving my appointment, Sophie once again came alive in my mind. Her presence was welcome, reassuring, and no matter whether she was real or a construct as the doctors had alluded to, the beautiful image of her lived on and burned ever so brightly.

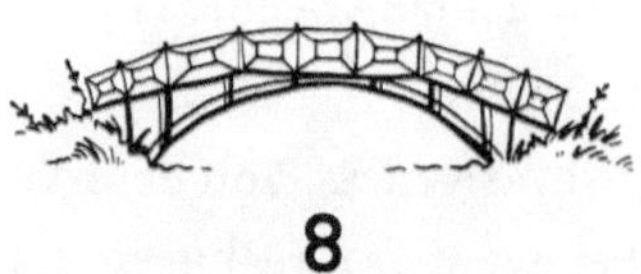

8

began to find comfort again in my old routine—for good or ill—although flipping through channels on the television and staying up late was not a productive use of my time. I was experiencing an odd restlessness, plus some unexpected feelings of anger. I thought it was gone, but it remained, resurrecting itself like an old wound that continued to impose itself upon my life without warning. Maybe the counseling had got me thinking about my past, and all those old thoughts, insecurities, and self-doubts that still weren't resolved.

I was feeling better physically, and what remained of a sore side or bruised rib had pretty much gone. For the most part, my memory seemed intact, but trying to understand who Sophie was, or if she even existed, remained a nagging mystery. Trying to put this jigsaw puzzle back together left me feeling agitated and anxious, and despite acknowledging what was happening to me, there was an element of obsession that was pushing at me, demanding that I continue the search for this mystery woman.

Why was I still so unsettled about this image of a woman who may or may not be real? I couldn't let it go, and I began to wonder if the accident had impaired my memory or recall to the extent that other important memories had gotten lost. Yet, every other aspect of my thinking and recall seemed intact. The feelings of isolation and such that I had been struggling with for some time were still there, but hopefully, my meetings with Olivia would support me to make positive changes. I did fear however, that this obsession to unravel the mystery of my dream girl would not stop, as her face, her words and her lively character continued to occupy my thinking. It would be my secret for now, tucked away with all those feelings I had so conveniently kept locked up from others.

As I sat and thought of it all, I decided it was best to follow Olivia's lead, and explore other elements within the narrative and see how they were linked, as there had been some past life matters that had been resurrected because of this experience. Maybe Olivia was right—this could be my chance to explore what had been hidden away for too long.

I had become lax about my exercise routine since the accident, and had confined myself to simple stretching and walking around my local area. But the desire to run again had returned. I was ready and anxious to get started again, and I was hopeful that this part of my routine might result in a healthier mindset.

"Think of analogies," Olivia had said to me, "because they can be powerful tools in understanding and stating our perspective."

So, as I sat back one evening, I imagined a scenario, and took her advice. I was crossing a deep river gorge on an old rope bridge with only wooden slats beneath my feet, and only weathered rope handles along the sides to hold onto. The bridge was swaying from side to side, and yet I felt the need to make it over. Fear, hesitation, having to take risks, wanting to turn back, getting stuck and unable to move—these thoughts were all there. But I was confident that, if I could make it over, there would be somebody there waiting to greet me—somebody to offer a comforting hand and to say hello once again.

Maybe, hopefully.

AUGUST HAD PROVEN TO be a somewhat rainy, yet still rather balmy, month. I yearned to feel the sun. Fortunately, my running regime was back in place, and I was once again making my way around my neighborhood, energized by my evening excursions, and finding security in the satisfying physical routine.

My work life was good, but in spite of the flexibility it offered me, there was still a complacency that characterized my routine. It was demanding work—deadlines, interviews, and such—and it left me feeling squeezed, unable to find the energy for my own writing projects that I had once deemed a priority. In the past I had briefly explored what it might be like to be a full-time freelance journalist, but had put that idea away, worried about the risks involved.

My career with North Star was flourishing, and my role as a feature writer with *Narrator* certainly had its benefits. Though I didn't make the money I would have hoped for working at North Star—not as much as I felt I deserved for all my long hours and hard work—I knew that was a reality of the profession. Money was not always a great motivator for me, as having purpose and passion for the work I did was always my top priority. A lofty ideal, since I had no desire to find myself chained to the proverbial desk, working a job that brought me little satisfaction. Often, I had entertained the idea of finding my way back to the US, working for a magazine or newspaper near Chicago—but for the time being I was satisfied living in England. On occasion I did write features for some of the other North Star magazines, working out of their London offices.

Still, since moving to the city, I had felt myself hiding away, going through the motions of a life without much investment in the world around me. Maybe the accident had done one thing for me—it seemed to refocus my thinking, and especially after the visit from my mother and sister, it began to make me appreciate all those beautiful things that bring our lives meaning.

AS MY LIFE BECAME clearer, the need to address the issues working against me started to take center stage. It would take effort and discipline, but I refused to let idleness occupy me, and instead tried to lay out a constructive plan of what I wanted my life to be like. It was difficult acknowledging that I needed support, but I was still young, and I didn't want to become caught in a loop that would prove detrimental to my growth. As a result, I began to read and watch content about people who had challenged their own static mindsets. It was these people that began to inspire me, as they ventured on in life taking risks, learning lessons along the way, and all the while growing and developing as they discovered new meaning.

Still, Sophie remained. There weren't many days when I didn't think of her, and whenever I did it felt like an indulgence. As I sat one evening and dwelled upon her, I decided for the most part not to speak of her anymore to those around me. I didn't want to appear obsessed, and make them worry about me.

As I sat back on my sofa, I let my mind wander back to my dream. I thought of her beautiful face, her voice, her smile, her laughter and what seemed to be a very few intimate moments we shared together. Yet, it wasn't real. I read my journal again and the words I used to describe her, and during those moments of indulgence, it allowed me the space to find respite—a place I could go to again where it was safe, warm, and reassuring.

As I sat and thought of Sophie, so many questions ran through my mind—questions that may never be answered, yet it was clear to me no attempt to rid my mind of her endearing face and lively spirit was going to be effective, because real or not, she was there somewhere, waiting to be discovered. I thus gave myself permission to go on this mind quest, remembering Sophie and reminding myself that there was value in this search, no matter how disappointing the outcome may be in the end.

That night, as garden rain sounds emanated from my small living room speakers, a pleasant wave of relaxation washed over me, and as I slowly began to drift off to sleep, I thought of her face and heard her voice once again, and wondered if she was out there.

Goodnight Sophie, sweet dreams.

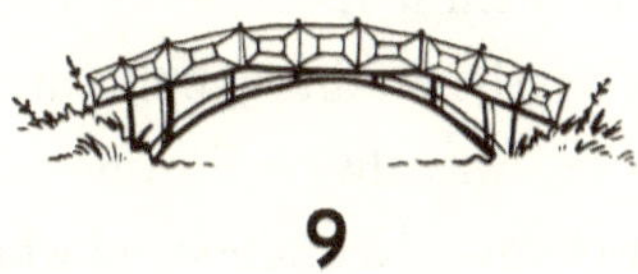

9

I sat in Olivia's office feeling relaxed, and appreciating the fact that I was beginning to speak more about myself without feeling uncomfortable or having to explain who I was.

Olivia listened patiently, and would sometimes share her insights or provide me with encouragement to elaborate on what I was thinking or feeling. She did it nicely, never forcing an issue, simply waiting until the right moment to make her move. It worked, and I was beginning to share things I never thought I would have with others.

During this appointment, I started by sharing my current state of mind, how work was going, plus thoughts about the process of my so-called reinvention, and how those around me might begin to see a different person.

Olivia nodded before replying, "Can you tell me what you think people might see when they look at you? Who is this person they're looking at now? What's he like? Can you describe yourself to me?"

It took me some time to come up with something. My answer to her question proved to be a rather trite array of generic personality traits—quiet, nice, trusting, caring, dependable, sensitive to others— and when I finished, I smiled at my feeble attempt to best describe myself. Instead, I ended up sounding like a used-car salesperson, trying to convince the customer why they should buy into it all.

While it was an accurate description of myself, it didn't touch on the struggle that had raged within me for a long time. Those other key words such as isolation, sadness, loneliness, anger, anxiety, withdrawal—none of them made it into my top ten—and it was apparent that Olivia clearly saw through this. It was difficult talking about myself, because I was always the one asking the questions of others, wanting to know and understand what made them tick. Yet as I sat with Olivia, I realized I was finding it difficult to answer those very same questions about myself, struggling with it all as I simply didn't feel that what I had to say really mattered.

"Can you tell me a little more?" Olivia asked with a kind smile.

"Well, I don't know. I like to run and read. I don't know. I guess I have a tendency to ask people a lot of questions about themselves, trying to learn about somebody—especially if we've just met. Maybe it's got something to do with my job, because I do a lot of that. But I'm genuinely interested in people, so I do like to know about people."

Olivia was quick to jump in, asking, "Why do you think you question people?"

"Well, I guess I just enjoy knowing what makes people who they are. I think that's what's difficult about our relationship, because it's hard to sit here and talk about myself, as I have a lot I would like to ask you, but I understand how this all works. You're the one who asks the questions. So, I don't know."

Olivia was persistent.

"Think on this a little more. Why do you question people? It was an interesting word you chose."

I paused for a long time without speaking. Olivia sat waiting as I ran it over in my mind, before she finally stepped in, breaking the uncomfortable silence.

"Do you think you ask all those questions, so that you can avoid others asking you about yourself? Avoidance can be a powerful tool sometimes. Don't talk about yourself—people don't get to know you. Were you always like that?"

As Olivia spoke, I could feel my old defenses falling into place.

"I'm not sure. I suppose if you reveal too much about yourself, then you expose yourself too much, and people might have an advantage over you, like you with me. You ask, you probe, you have the advantage over me in some respects."

"Well, help me out here. What advantage do I have over you? I mean, yes, it's my job to try and understand where you are at, but I don't consider it an advantage."

"Well, in this relationship, there's a power imbalance. I think my father was a bit reserved and didn't share a lot, and I think I'm like that as well. I don't like to commit myself to friendships necessarily. I mean I have one close friend, kind of, and other acquaintances, but I can be a bit of a loner. Maybe it's as simple as that."

Olivia was letting me flounder, and suddenly I felt at a loss for words. How could someone like me be lost for words? I also noticed I was playing with my pen, disassembling and reassembling it over and over. I felt uncomfortable and when I finally shifted my attention from my pen over to Olivia, her gaze unsettled me—she wasn't allowing me to crawl out of this self-made ravine I had fallen into. I felt compelled to find more to say, to fill the silence, and I became unnerved by it all.

"I guess I just think sometimes, if we don't reveal too much, then it's easier to maintain relationships without all the complication."

Olivia looked puzzled, and asked, "What does that mean?"

"Well, I think I approach all things in my life in a pragmatic way. I handle adversity well and avoid placing myself in uncomfortable situations with others, and I think people know that about me."

"Do you think you handle things in a pragmatic and mature manner, because it allows you to not feel sometimes?"

"I don't know." I laughed out loud in exasperation. "I'm not even sure what I'm saying makes any sense, and I feel like I'm rambling."

Olivia nodded.

"Okay. Sometimes it's a difficult task to talk about ourselves. I'm going to assume something here. I'm just not sure when you're with people just maybe the inner self stays hidden away and doesn't always come out and involve itself. Relationships can make us feel vulnerable, but that's okay sometimes. You felt vulnerable today, because you didn't know where it was going, and that's unsettling."

It had been an awkward session, but one that proved insightful to me, and upon further reflection it forced me to answer a few of those questions I had avoided for so long. Before I left, I shared my rope bridge analogy with Olivia. She liked it, and of course, she couldn't let it pass without adding something.

"You know, seems like you're out there on that bridge right now, and maybe have been for a while. It might feel that way to you. But you know what? You don't have to cross that bridge on your own, and you don't even have to cross that bridge if it doesn't feel right. It's okay asking for help and having a little support to get you over, if you do choose to cross it. It doesn't make you any less courageous or weak or any of that."

Despite my struggles in this session, Olivia's insights were brilliant, and despite my resistance at times, there was something reassuring and safe sitting with her for those fifty minutes. I would return next week, and I was confident now that Olivia would be waiting eagerly.

When September rolled around, the responsibility of work was keeping me occupied. I was back in the flow and with a calendar full of appointments and work assignments, the routine of my existence remained unchanged. Autumn was an inspiring time for me, more so when I lived in the States, but I still appreciated the transition from summer into the crisp temperatures that often characterized this time.

My running regime was firmly back in place—generally a solitary experience, other than the occasional run I shared with Flynn, as we ran around the streets of Greenwich, chatting about whatever crossed our minds at the time. Very often on a weekend run, we would make our way to Greenwich Park, ending our run by sitting at the small café in the park drinking Americanos, putting the world to rights. I always found this aspect of our relationship comforting, a small stopover from the everyday demands life asks of us all.

It felt good having some structure in my life, as it often proved helpful in keeping myself organized and on task with both work and personal duties. However, thanks to my newfound sense of self-awareness, due in no small part to my work with Olivia, I had begun to make changes in my life—moving towards living a healthier lifestyle, which included eating better and attending to my exercise routine. Running was an important part of my life, however I wanted to ensure that it was a constructive part of my life too, not just an addictive behavior to fill the time. I wanted to enjoy the experience, and not worry about outcomes—how far I ran on a particular evening, for example, or how I would squeeze a run in on a busy day. I didn't want any of that to matter anymore.

In the past, I had joined a running club in my local area. I met some people, did the runs, and even ran the London Marathon alongside members of the club. But eventually I fell away from it all, because I couldn't seem to merge the whole social contact thing with running. The camaraderie was nice, but it began to become more than running, with evening and Saturday socials. It just wasn't for me. I met my ex-partner Julia Watts during a charity run in London, so I guess finding common ground could indeed bring people together.

But I lost my zest for the running collectives, and fell back into my safe routine. I left those connections behind and began to enjoy and relish the solitude of my runs. It was my time, and valuing the spirit of the run was all that made sense to me in the end. The September evenings were beginning to offer me solace. I suppose in some respects I was still hiding, yet I pushed on, running through neighborhoods I knew well, and down familiar streets that oddly brought me comfort, while savoring the sense of liberation and the freedom of choice.

ONE VERY LATE AND dark September evening, I ran through a wet mist that covered everything, and brought a chill to me as I ventured through darkened streets. Once back at home, I took a long hot shower, devoured a makeshift dinner, switched on my laptop, and settled in with the best intentions of doing some late-night work. But my wandering mind had other plans for me, and instead I sat and stared into space, trying to decide whether to close the laptop and get on with something else, or scroll through the internet looking for new running shoes. On this evening, neither option prevailed, and instead my focus switched to Sophie—she was always there in my thoughts, living on, her voice playing in my head, securing me to this one place where I would not forget or dismiss those valuable memories.

That evening, I searched the internet as I had done many times in the past, typing in everything I could think of into the search engine—Sophie, France, organizational consultants, Nice, flowers, every possible little fact and bit of information that I could remember. I must have typed the name Sophie into my search engine over a hundred times, but with just a first name I was coming up empty.

My search soon became limited to French sites, trying somehow to find the needle in my self-constructed haystack. I even attempted to review directories such as the *Pages Jaunes* that might shed some light on my search. I looked through French cities and towns, but typing in the name Sophie over and over proved an endless, frustrating task. It yielded so many results, and yet nothing rang familiar.

I focused on Nice, typed the name Sophie in and reviewed what results came up—but still it was hopeless—nothing worked without a last name, a birth date, or any other identifying factor. A first name wasn't enough, and out of desperation, I even looked through census information and civil registration, anything that might yield some answers. But after so many hours in front of the screen, and recognizing the enormity of such a fruitless task, I felt it was time to surrender. Maybe at some point it was there in front of me, and I just simply missed it—it was impossible to tell. What I did discover was the frustration and angst growing inside of me because of my endless searching.

Before leaving my search however, and out of total desperation, I searched my phone once again for some discreet clue within a photo, a message—anything I may have overlooked. Despite feeling exasperated, I remained persistent, yet nothing revealed itself to me. I even went back to my laptop and made a mad attempt to look up businesses in Nice, scouring more phone directories, everything I could think of. I was a reporter and thus prided myself on being able to discover things that were often hidden from view, feeling that there was something I must have been overlooking. But nothing seemed to work.

By the time I finished my search, it was the very early hours of the morning, and I had spent four fruitless hours in front of my laptop. I was exhausted and had nothing to show for my efforts. This wasn't the first search I had undertaken, and it wouldn't be the last. I began to feel like one of those internet detectives, and then had the somewhat mad idea of enlisting help from a professional. Yet I had the skills, the knack for finding those who are discreetly hidden amongst the many pages of internet searches. I had convinced myself that she must be out there, and I wouldn't stop looking.

Unfortunately, this futile effort had worn me out, ground me down, and continued to taunt me, leaving me feeling downtrodden. I began to accept that my investigatory skills weren't all that impressive, although I had done a fair amount of digging when it came to researching articles. But I was getting nowhere with this search, and realistically could anyone hope to discover anything if all they had was a first name? Possibly, through some social media connection, yet who knows how long I would have to search before I found what I was looking for, or what the results of that might yield? It was only a whimsical idea that swirled through my head, this wayward thought of finding a woman in a dream, and if and when I did find her—maybe there'd be nothing. Perhaps just the satisfaction of knowing I found what I was looking for, no matter what the outcome of that discovery might be, would have to be enough. The idea that I had possibly come upon her through one of my many searches began to play on my mind, because maybe I had found her but dismissed it because it didn't ring familiar to me, or I was simply too tired to take notice. It was hard to say. So much searching and scrolling through masses of information, and somewhere amongst it all, those elusive answers may have been staring me in the face all along.

My thoughts even turned to the possibility of spending some time in Nice, maybe a long weekend trip. I could sit in Garibaldi Square, hoping to catch a glimpse of this mystery woman, or I could explore library and civic records on the ground, anything that might help me unravel the mystery. But the pragmatic and sensible side of me said it didn't make sense—a random trip to the south of France to seek out a woman who remained only an image in my mind sounded like a fruitless exercise.

I packed up my computer for the night, sat back and reluctantly accepted the fact that maybe this entire search was futile. Even if I did miraculously find this woman, how did I know she was who she really was? What outcome was I truly seeking—finding her through some quirk of good fortune, and then what? Or would I merely end up wasting time and emotional energy chasing some desperate image or construct that I had created in my mind to appease the emptiness in my own life?

This mental tug-of-war was tearing me apart, creating an obsessive pattern of search and find, intruding upon my mental space, holding me captive and preventing me from getting on with the business of life. I didn't know how to free myself from it all, other than simply dismissing the thought whenever it slipped into my wandering mind.

If only it was that easy.

10

I t was always inside of me from a very young age—that sense of
spontaneity, impulsiveness, impatience. I don't know if people are
born with these attributes, or if they just acquire them as they move
through the many layers of life. But I knew it was there inside of
me, spurring me onward, disregarding the logic of a planned life.

By the time I had reached my teens, I had become averse
and intolerant when presented with anything that was planned,
scheduled, or carefully arranged ahead of time, especially those
life events that seemingly demanded my participation. It felt like a
sense of control over my own life was being compromised. Unlike
my parents and sister, who were ardent planners and schedulers,
I was the daydreamer, choosing to let things fall as they were. But
then, where would the world be without organizers and planners?

As I got older, and despite gaining an appreciation for the need
for organization and planning in my life, that inner desire to rebel
against such rigidity and conformity remained. No matter what the
occasion, anything from a vacation to a run in the park, I simply
had an aversion to forward planning.

Unfortunately, this somewhat unstructured mindset did not
mesh well with the working world, and too often I found myself
reliant upon my paper-based appointment book to navigate my way
through the professional environment. Hence, this odd tug-of-war

between order and spontaneity continued inside of me. As a result, and despite my eventual place within the regimented hierarchy of life, there were those moments when strict protocol would be abandoned, and a strong sense of impulsiveness and whimsy would guide me onward.

WHICH MORE THAN LIKELY explains why, at this juncture, I found myself in Nice, France, sipping on a very welcome strong coffee under a warm sun in Garibaldi Square. Yes, I gave in to my obsession, and despite my best efforts to clear my mind of the persistent images and thoughts of this mysterious young French woman, I convinced myself that a few relaxing days in Nice might not be such a bad thing. This trip, this plan was strictly clandestine, hatched very quickly on Thursday evening following my appointment with Olivia. I had to find the truth about the mysterious Sophie, and with spontaneity pushing me onward, a three-day trip to Nice was planned within minutes. Nobody could know I had done this. The thought of never discovering who she was and where she lived haunted me, and with little to base this search upon, I packed a small bag and boarded my flight. I was determined to find something, an answer possibly, or just maybe a small clue that might lead me onward.

It was Saturday morning, around eleven, and I was seated at that same coffee shop that I remembered so very well. I remember sitting here in this very spot when I came with Flynn and Emily so many years ago now. Also, the same spot I remember in a long and mysterious dream. The sun kindly warmed my body and soul, and as I glanced about this busy French square, I convinced myself that on this day, I would find an answer. There was nothing to go on—no evidence, clues, other than a beautiful face and spirit that came alive in my dream, so it was strictly a shot in the dark, a hunch, and a spontaneous spirit to lead me onward. There was no idea or plan as to how best to investigate this mystery, and what I did undertake was quite unimaginative—walking around Nice's old town, visiting the market, hoping to see something that might trigger my memory. Sophie was here, she had to be, and with some luck, maybe I would see her somewhere—in the market possibly, shopping for some little treasure that would make her day that much brighter. It seemed fitting.

I had an early stroll down the Cours Saleya, watching closely as all sorts of visitors to the market passed by my line of sight. I walked along the Promenade des Anglais, staring out at the Mediterranean for the most part, yet keeping my eyes peeled for any resemblance of a certain young woman who might just be enjoying a relaxing Saturday stroll. But no such luck. So, I headed off to Garibaldi Square to sit and observe. Despite my lack of success thus far, there was still an odd sense of optimism that gave me reason for hope. I had no agenda, nobody to answer to, and if I so chose, I could sit as long as I wanted and just maybe, my patience and determination to solve this mystery might be rewarded.

After some time, I felt another coffee was in order. Upon getting my waiter Antoine's attention, he wandered over my way, offering me a broad smile. Fortunately for me, my initial attempt to order coffee using my best French was only successful after Antoine informed me he spoke English. So being the lazy linguist, I felt fortunate to be rescued in that moment by my gracious and considerate waiter. He had been so friendly to me, I decided to introduce myself.

"By the way, I'm Mike. Thanks for your positive spirit. Very much appreciated."

"Well Mike, glad to be of service. So, is your stay in Nice for business or pleasure?"

"Just visiting again. A tourist I guess."

"So, you've been here before?"

"Yeah, I came with friends before. And I've got a bit of a frivolous reason for coming this time, kind of a whim. I live in England, so, it's just a short flight."

"So, are you here alone then? I could recommend some nice places to visit if that would help?"

"Thanks Antoine. I appreciate your offer, but I am actually looking for someone, or hoping to see someone, would be more like it."

"Oh, I see."

Antoine's puzzled look told me he deserved an explanation.

"It's complicated. I came looking for a girl who I met at this very place, at your fine establishment. I met her and had a drink with her here, went for a stroll, and well, circumstances were such that I only got her first name and she had to leave. Kind of nonsensical I know, but I came back hoping to find her."

Antoine looked thoughtful, as if searching for just the right thing to say to me.

"Wow, what was this girl like? What did she look like? Maybe she comes here."

"Well, that's what I was hoping, that just maybe if I sat here long enough, she might make an appearance. Her name was Sophie— about my age, dark hair, lovely face, slim, soothing and alluring voice, great dress sense—did I say beautiful?"

Antoine looked down at me and nodded his head.

"Well as you know, France has some of the most beautiful women in the world. Unfortunately, your description fits many. I wish I could be more help."

I thanked Antoine for his kind sentiment and ordered a Croque Monsieur and yet another coffee, mostly out of guilt for taking his time. And with my order in hand, Antoine went on his way.

When Antoine returned with my food, he seemed determined to help me solve my mystery. I couldn't tell him that all this mad scenario came to me in a dream, so I had to keep playing along with my own ruse.

"Can I ask you something—this woman that you are searching for, did you say she lived here in Nice?"

"Yeah, she lives here. She has a house. I remember her telling me that."

"Well, I'm not an expert, but I am sure there are places to look. There are records and, how do you say, the town hall. I could direct you there if you wish. You seemed determined to find this woman. She must be special. I mean, first impressions and all. If this woman took you back here to Nice, then the search must be worth it. I did ask my colleagues if they knew of a woman named Sophie who visits here, but they didn't know anyone. I think maybe if we had more to go on…"

"Antoine, I appreciate your kindness. Let's see where we go from here."

When I finished my meal and Antoine delivered my cheque, I thanked him and left him a hearty tip for all his efforts. As he began to walk away, I requested his attention one more time.

"One other thing Antoine. Sophie—she likes flowers of all kinds. Snapdragons, however, are her favorite. That much I know."

Antoine looked over and smiled, saying, "Have a good day my friend. Maybe I'll see you tomorrow." As he started on his way, he stopped suddenly. "I have an idea. Why don't you give me your phone number, because if a beautiful, dark-haired, alluring French woman comes along carrying some flowers, well, you never know. I'm sorry you've lost your friend—I wish I could do more for you."

Before he turned away, Antoine paused for a moment, seemingly to collect his thoughts.

"May I share something with you?"

I nodded, curious as to what Antoine was about to tell me.

"One day, about a year ago, my cat went missing, and myself and my girlfriend were both very upset. She was almost two years old when she went missing. She was given to me by my sister. I named her Brigitte, and she was just a little kitten when my sister gave her to me. Anyway, she went missing one day, and was gone for almost seven days. I thought she was gone, disappeared, vanished, even worse maybe. I looked everywhere, made up posters and put them around. Friends helped me search. We looked and looked but couldn't find her."

"Then one night after work, I came home and was opening the front door, and suddenly out of the blue came Brigitte. No idea where she had been. But there she was, walking right back into my life, and she has been with me ever since. So, who knows about life? Strange, but brilliant things happen. Who knows? Anyway, good day my friend."

I thanked Antoine and did indeed give him my phone number, because one never knows what might just lie around the next corner.

As I walked away from the restaurant, I thought of Antoine's cat story and smiled. Maybe it was a peculiar analogy, but I understood why he shared it. Like many who take the time and make an effort to invest in others, the simple intent of trying to provide a sense of optimism and hope is commendable. Antoine reached into his bag of consideration and pulled out a story of hope. His efforts did not go unnoticed.

Thinking of my return to life in London, I truly hoped that I wouldn't pass others by without taking notice and missing those small windows of opportunity to offer encouragement and a sense of hope.

The rest of my day was fueled by my incessant, meandering spirit, as I wandered around Nice in an aimless yet determined manner. I liked it—my eyes open, searching, hoping that maybe Sophie might come walking my way.

In the early evening, I put on my running attire and headed out, striding through the busy streets of Nice, moving along with ease and a comfortable pace, enjoying the sights. I finally ended my run along the Promenade des Anglais where I found a bench to sit on and watch life go by, as I listened to the rhythmic sounds of the Mediterranean. I felt relaxed and found myself sitting for over an hour before I headed back to my hotel.

After showering and scanning the internet for a bit, I headed out for the evening, finding a lovely restaurant close to the old town. L'usine Alimentaire proved to be the most incredible seafood restaurant I had ever encountered. For almost two hours, I sat alone at my table, staring out the nearby window, enjoying every mouthful, while still hoping to catch a glimpse of a mysterious yet familiar face in the crowd.

After dinner I took a long walk, taking in the refreshing evening air, watching others as they strolled through the sunlit streets, some holding hands or walking arm in arm, enjoying the sights and sounds of this lovely French city.

On Sunday, I started my day with a determined spirit. In the morning, I sat outside the restaurant from my dream in Garibaldi Square, in my very same seat, hoping my early adventure might yield something hopeful. Antoine was nowhere in sight, and as I sipped away at my coffee and nibbled at my tasty croissant, I jotted down ideas and strategies that might help me in my search. I came up with an action plan of sorts, including new avenues to search, even mulling the prospect of putting some internet-based message in a bottle out there.

I did much the same as I did on Saturday, walking around the old town, being diligent about what was happening around me. The day proved uneventful in most respects, other than the fact that I found a cool cat mug at one of the unique gift shops, thinking Antoine might appreciate it. My evening was much the same as the last—a relaxing jog around Nice, back to the hotel for a shower, and then out for an evening dinner.

My flight out of Nice on Monday was in the late afternoon. I arose early and went for a wander. I bought a blank card with a cat on it, wrote a note to Antoine and wrapped his mug in some paper I found, adorned with bright balloons of every color. On my way to the restaurant, I happened to come upon the Saint-Martin-Saint-Augustin Church along Place Saint-Augustin. I had passed this church on previous strolls around the old town, but had simply wandered on by without paying much attention. Today, as I was passing by, a woman exited the church through the front doors.

My curiosity got the best of me and as I made my way inside, the coolness and soothing quiet presented a welcome contrast to the very warm temperatures and busy streets outside its heavy front doors. A small leaflet said that the church was built in 1837 and was of the Baroque style. The church was also declared a historical monument in 1946. It made me wonder how many people entered the church without consideration of its interesting past.

The church was empty for the most part, dimly lit with just a few people sitting about, either resting or engaging in private worship, and I found a seat in one of the many chairs lined up together in neat rows, forming an aisle leading up to the altar. The inside was beautiful, and after I had glanced around at the fascinating architecture, I settled in and appreciated the sense of calm that had begun to permeate my spirit. My first thoughts were always about those individuals who built these incredible churches and cathedrals. How did they do it? How did they manage to build such magnificence, so detailed, elegant, yet so immensely powerful? I allowed my body and mind to relax, trying desperately to clear my head and just simply live in the moment—feeling the coolness, the calming atmosphere of this spiritual place wash over me. I closed my eyes for just a short time, appreciating the quiet and solemn nature of all that surrounded me. As I stared toward the front of the church, a Catholic priest walked up the middle aisle in my direction. As he got near, we made eye contact and he quietly greeted me, not wanting to disrupt my contemplation.

As he came close to me, he smiled and nodded in greeting. I smiled back and reciprocated his greeting. It's interesting how those brief little moments, when we meet and greet someone passing by, who we will probably never see again in our life, can stick in the memory. I truly believe there is a connecting point with others, where one can leave an impression upon another, no matter how insignificant their shared contact may be.

I eventually made my way out of the church and headed down to La Fleur Bleue, my go-to place for people-watching and my seat of hope while searching for the elusive Sophie. I was told Antoine was starting later today, so I left the mug and the card and asked if they would kindly hand it to him when he reported in for work. My note to Antoine was simple: an acknowledgment to him for taking the time to give me a ray of hope.

Dear Antoine, You will have to endure my poor command of the French language and vocabulary once again, hence my written note being in English. I wanted to thank you for the kindness and consideration you offered me on Saturday. Your kind words truly made a difference to me. My search hasn't ended, and your words of encouragement and hope, that in part, will keep me going. Best wishes to you, your girlfriend, and Brigitte. I was so glad to hear that your furry friend found her way back to you. Your story was most appreciated and very inspiring, truly. All the best. Take care. Mike

My flight back to London was smooth and uneventful. Tomorrow life would resume, and this secret search in Nice would be my story to tell another day, maybe. For now, it would remain my secret, this excursion of fancy, back to a place where this mysterious and beautiful dream-girl came to life.

As I sat on the plane, I felt neither disappointment nor discouragement—I didn't have massive expectations, and this whimsical adventure gave me a chance to take better control of a situation that continued to mystify me and leave me without answers or insights. Maybe none of it was real, just a dream indeed, an image simply created by a lonely mind or a lost soul. But then, why the face, the name, the beautiful French accent, and a dream of time spent with this enchanting, unforgettable young woman?

However, for now it was time to move on with life. I had other challenges to face, decisions to make and a future life that demanded my attention, and it was time to focus on all that which was real and tangible.

Real life was waiting.

11

I arrived at my appointment with Olivia in a relaxed mood. My previous session focused on what I deemed my reinvention process, and Olivia had been curious and asked what I thought the key factors were when someone was trying to 'reinvent' themselves. Why does someone seek to reinvent themselves? What was involved? How does one mark progress or determine if the process was working? And it is even necessary for one to reinvent oneself at all to create positive change?

The session had a positive, optimistic slant to it, and I laughed more than usual and spoke about my work, my running, my new priorities in terms of my family, my leisure time, and future goals both career and personal. Discussion around the dream narrative that I had experienced in the hospital was put aside for the time being. I thought maybe Olivia was just allowing me to go where I wanted, but little did I realize that we would come back to this mad narrative in our next session.

"Mike, I wanted to ask you about work. Can you tell me when you came to England after college? I'd like to better understand that."

I wasn't quite sure about the relevance of her question, but Olivia seemed interested. I explained that we remained in London until I was 17. My sister had returned to the States to attend university. We then relocated back to Ravenswood, my father resumed his work back in Chicago, and my mother went back to her work as well.

Olivia stopped me again.

"Mike, could you tell me again what your father did for a living?"

"Well, my father was very intelligent and was an actuary for an international insurance company, hence the reason for our move to London. He requested a return to Chicago when I was older, and so we moved back and he became a supervisor, but still did a fair amount of traveling."

Olivia was interested in knowing more, and I began to feel quite anxious about her persistence.

"What happened to you when you returned to Chicago?"

"So, well I…well in short, I attended Northwestern University, got a degree in journalism, and afterward worked in Chicago doing some writing. Eventually I got a job with North Star Media and worked in Chicago a while longer, before moving to London."

Olivia was clearly focused on what I was saying and seemed intent on getting a better understanding of times and dates.

"So, did you start work for your current magazine right away? And how old were you when you came back here?"

"Ummm, yeah, I started to write for the magazine when I came here. I also wrote features for some of their other publications, and still do on occasion. I was 25, I think."

"Why did you move back here?"

"Well, the job opportunity, and I liked London. I mean, I kept in contact with Flynn and saw him at different times when I lived back in Chicago, and I just wanted to give it a try on my own I guess."

"Quite a big decision to just pick up and move like that."

I sat without saying anything, unsure if Olivia expected a response or not. She peered at me and said nothing for a few moments before breaking the silence.

"Your father resumed his work in Chicago and your mother went back to work, when you all returned. How was life then? What were things like when you were in college and all?"

"It was good for the most part."

"Okay. Well, you told me when we were speaking about your dream that your father died in an accident. How old were you? And can you tell me your father's name again?"

"My father's name was William, or Will as he preferred to be called. I was almost 22, and still in college. My dad was 53 when he died."

"Do you remember that time well?"

"Yeah, of course. It was a shock to us—my mother, sister, and me. Out of the blue."

I could feel my head lower, and I was powerless to control the emotions that were beginning to swirl about within. I was struggling as the self-control that I had relied on in the past had abandoned me in my time of need. I remained unsettled, anxious, and unsure of what to say. Olivia was persistent and pushed at me.

"Can we talk about your father's death?"

I hesitated, but felt Olivia deserved an answer. I had spoken of my father in fragments to others, but nothing in depth—even to Olivia. Most people were always very willing to back off when it was clear I was changing the direction of the conversation. Olivia, however, refused to back down.

Thinking of my father's death was something I rarely did. Even in the company of my mother and sister, it was rare that we discussed the circumstances of it. Olivia continued to look at me. My pen in hand, I was clearly not in a place to do this.

"Your father had a part in your dream, and maybe it might help us if we take some time to talk about him—it may open that dream narrative a bit and help us understand a little more about it. Does that make sense?"

And so I began to tell Olivia the story of my father's death, a senseless and brutal event.

A work conference brought him to Cleveland, Ohio during a cold and snowy January. He was presenting a workshop on tools and systems at a regional data management meeting.

Some weeks before the conference, arrangements had been made for me to stay with my father in Cleveland—leaving on the Wednesday, and returning on Sunday. He had invited me along and, after some consideration, I had agreed to it all, with him saying we'd have the Friday afternoon and all day Saturday and part of Sunday to wander around Cleveland together. He was excited that I had accepted his invite, and had already made plans for us to attend the Rock and Roll Hall of Fame and the Museum of Art, plus had scoped out a couple of restaurants that we might both enjoy.

I was in the midst of an independent work study, and finding time to spend with my father seemed like a good thing to do. There was nothing holding me back, with the only obstacle being an over-focus on my own immediate needs, as had been for some time.

It had been a long while since I had spent time with my father on a one-to-one basis. Throughout my younger years, we did spend a lot of time together, but as I got older, I began to spend less and less time with him, drifting away from him in some respects, as my own life began to take shape. We used to watch sports on television, share vacations, and just enjoy being together, but I didn't live at home now and the freedom of being involved in college life kept me away. He used to ask me to go fishing with him on occasion, but I was always too busy to do something so mundane—at least that's what I used to tell him—and so he would simply accept my decision and instead spend those weekends watching sports on television or working around the house, helping my mother with the usual tasks and chores that were a part of their routine. On the odd occasion that he did go fishing, he would pack his poles and various gear into his old Ford pick-up and head off on his own, hoping to sit on a sunny bank somewhere and enjoy whatever peace and quiet he could find.

We had agreed that spending some time together on this trip was long overdue, and would give us a chance to be together for a couple of days without the demands of everyday life hanging over our heads.

However, as the day of our departure grew nearer, I searched my mind for any reason I could use to drop out. There was no overriding reason compelling me to stay back, other than the lure of hanging out with some college chums and heading out to some local bars. So, I made my excuses, telling my father that some work and study commitments had come up and I would not be able to make it. He accepted it all, as he did so many times in the past, but this time with noticeable disappointment in his voice.

Truth be told, I simply couldn't be bothered to go—instead choosing to indulge my own immediate needs, disregarding the opportunity to spend time with my beautiful father. Oddly enough, for so long, I told myself that opportunities to spend quality time with my parents and sister would come one day. I told myself that over and over, never truly understanding that those times were already available to me, but I simply couldn't be bothered. My sister was a brilliant daughter to both my mother and father, always making her relationship with them a priority, always finding the time to be with them, no matter what life threw at her.

I teased my father before he left on his trip, asking him about the type of people who would attend a data management meeting, sharing a few laughs on the phone and telling him I would see him when he got back.

On the Friday morning of the conference, my father walked through a sub-level car park, beneath the hotel where he was staying, and made his way up to a nondescript road, anxious to embark on one of his beloved morning walks. It was about seven in the morning as he made his way down this road, an area with a few small industrial businesses, and some unused construction and industrial equipment scattered around. He would then return to his room, get ready, and head off to the hotel conference suite.

However, during his morning stroll, my father's journey would be cut short. As he walked along, a 36-year-old man by the name of Randy Matson approached my father from the opposite direction. There was no way to know what was said, or even if anything was said. Matson produced—what police would discover later—a stolen handgun, and shot and killed my father. He appeared to have taken what little cash my father had in his wallet, and took the watch he wore, which had been presented to him by the company president for long service. Matson was seen running from the scene by an employee from a local construction business, situated along an intersecting street. He was caught by police a couple of weeks later, due in part to Matson's clumsy attempts to cover his own tracks, and thanks to the eyewitness who was able to identify him.

What else can one say about such a crime? Senseless and brutal.

My father was a dear man. A kind, brilliant man who loved his family, worked hard, enjoyed sports, and cherished nature. He was modest, humble, very unassuming, and was good to everyone he met. Above all he lived an honest life and was one of the most ethical, caring, and gentle individuals a person could ever know. On that day, it started with a simple morning walk, and ended with a fatal gunshot—destiny, fate, whatever one chooses to call it. For the police in Cleveland, my father became nothing more than another gun-related crime statistic.

For so very long, I had refused to think too deeply about it—when I did sit and think on it, the image I chose to conjure was one of my incredible father enjoying his morning walk. I tried not to think of what happened next. I couldn't think of it. By closing myself off to those dreadful memories, I was able to bury some of the pain and grief that lay in wait. However, the deep feelings of guilt were yet another matter. These were not excludable, and this unrelenting guilt became my tormentor, forcing me out into the margins of life, a deserving outcome for a son who had abandoned his father.

My story to Olivia was difficult to verbalize—once again, I was forced to confront that darkest of days, as I had so many times in the past. When the news reached me, my cowardly cancellation tore at me, and every disagreement, every time I was insensitive or mean to my father rushed into my head. The times I said no to his invitations to go fishing or to stay at home and watch a game with him began to haunt me. Those opportunities, those meaningful life moments and possibilities of sharing time together were now gone. I would have to live with that, and with this came the guilt and anger.

Olivia stared at me. My expression must have appeared empty, as I sat with a fixed gaze, finally unable to say anymore.

"I'm sorry Mike," she said, "I know how painful it must be to have to recall those events. Your father sounded like a wonderful man."

"Sometimes I can only remember the times when I upset him or said no to him when he wanted me around. If I had gone with him, there is a good chance he would still be alive. If I had been there, the course of his life would have played out differently—I could have stopped that terrible event from happening if we had walked together. I abandoned him and he died. I should have been at his side, but I couldn't be bothered. I was a selfish little prick, too busy with my own life to even give his life a thought, and…" But before I could finish, the tears came to me, and I stopped.

My world had made little sense since my father died. I had lived a life after that tragic event, but it had been an empty one.

I never wept, and instead allowed anger and guilt to become my companions—that same guilt would continue to haunt me daily, and the anger kept me apart from others. In the end, it was my anger that anesthetized me and prevented any helpful thought, emotion, or feeling from making its way into my life.

It was all true what Olivia had been saying, asking the questions, never thinking too deeply—I was one of those people she had described. Always keeping my mind going with something else, always distracting myself, going through the motions of a life. In the process however, I forgot how to live, feel, or care—and on this day, I wept for my father and for myself. I wept for his loss, for his life cut short, and I wept for all the sadness that had made its way into my life unnoticed.

Maybe I didn't deserve to feel grief. Grief should only be reserved for those who make the effort. I worried that maybe my father's last thoughts were about the son who left him out there on his own. And so—I stopped living, committed emotional suicide, and hid in any darkened recess I could find.

I wept and wept, and suddenly I blurted out through the tears, "I'm so sorry Dad." I felt myself shaking as my tears fell onto the floor, and I was alone again, running down those darkened streets, hiding and escaping from the reality that had haunted me for so very long. Olivia sat back quietly until I had stopped. I was exhausted, spent, and had nothing left in me.

I could sense Olivia's eyes upon me.

"Mike, people can often hold on to guilt when somebody they love dies. It becomes all about what we said, what we didn't say, what we should have said or done. We don't often remember the good things we said or shared. Love is a difficult concept to process and understand sometimes. It's expected that we will all experience grief in our lives at some time or another, but if we aren't careful, we can get stuck in it, and guilt is much the same. This self-blame that you carry around with you has kept you stuck, and grief and guilt have become your captors. None of what happened to your father was your fault—there are just bad things that happen in life."

We sat for some time in silence, until I finally was able to look up. Olivia sat back and appeared to be surveying the scene, and we continued sitting in silence until those moments of deep grief had passed.

However, something had happened in those moments as I told Olivia the story of my father's death. Despite her words of consolation, they went largely unheard. The moments of grief had now passed, but I felt angry at Olivia for tearing at me, for breaking down my place of hiding, and leaving me exposed and vulnerable. Olivia had seen through my thin wall of protection some time ago and waited for just the right moment to make her move and attack without warning. At least it felt that way to me. I didn't see it coming, I didn't expect it. I felt full of pain, emotionally immobilized, and as though I had nowhere to turn.

Olivia was concerned about my state of being, but I needed to leave this place today, to find a sense of respite somewhere out amidst the confusion of a busy city. I felt as though this sudden injection of pain and emotional turmoil occurred because in some respects, I had opened the door to a therapist who had forced me to abandon my haven, my protection, and relive the tragedy that had forced me into hiding, away from the reality of an event that had brought me to my knees. Despite Olivia's best attempts to keep me in her office, I was determined to leave and did my best to assure her that I would be back.

After the session, as I walked through the London streets, I felt scared, angry, and unprotected—images of my father played over and over in my mind, a reminder of a beautiful life I could have saved, if not for the selfish and errant mindset that had led me so far astray. There was an odd feeling within me as I walked on, unsure of what was to come. Life changed for me on that day, and when pain came to visit once again, I felt unprepared and was now left facing a new world, an unfamiliar one, as my defenses of old had been torn down during that fifty-minute counseling session.

As thoughts of my father continued to occupy my mind, I headed straight home as I was void of any willingness to seek resolve amidst the busy streets of London, or an office full of demands and endless deadlines. For the time being, I needed a refuge, a place to go where I could lock the doors, be alone, and prepare myself for what might still await me.

DESPITE MY TUMULTUOUS EMOTIONAL state, work continued to offer respite and stability. Still, one evening I found myself stuck in the office late at night, staring with tired eyes at a computer screen, wondering if it was all worth it.

At times, my job had become so entangled with my life outside of work, that the boundaries between the two became blurred, and my routine would fall out of balance. I valued my profession, but there were times I felt as though the job was swallowing me up, forcing me to live a lopsided existence, and my routine became a repetitive slog of work, running, eating, and what seemed like very little else.

During one of my sessions with Olivia, we talked about work briefly and something she said really stood out: "You know, you can like something a lot, but that doesn't always make it a good thing."

I had to earn a living and doing something I enjoyed made sense, but at what cost? For so long, I thought I had a good sense of knowing when to turn off the proverbial light switch and go home, but too often I found myself alone in that office or at home struggling to meet a deadline, thinking all along that I was bringing purpose to my life.

Unfortunately, I had ignored other parts of my life, justifying it all by saying I needed to make a living. It was one of life's dilemmas—liking a job but lacking the insight or willpower to turn off the light switch and walk away. Sticking with this routine had become my fix, another unhealthy life choice, as it became all too easy to hide behind the expectations and demands of a job.

I had contemplated for some time striking out on my own and becoming strictly freelance—however it felt daunting, and sticking with what I had was the easy thing to do. Yet the thought was still out there, and I was beginning to recognize the possibilities of what could be and what doors it may open—and so, ever so slightly, I began to feel those gusty winds of change starting to blow.

12

It was October and I was in Olivia's office, revisiting the dream narrative. I felt strange at times sitting with Olivia now, knowing how effectively she could dismantle my defenses. The pain of revelation concerning my father's death reminded me of my emotional vulnerabilities, and despite my reluctance at times to involve myself in this therapeutic endeavor, I recognized the importance of carrying on with it.

After our brief catch-up, Olivia got straight to the point today.

"I wanted to hear a bit about your ex-partner, because she seemed to have a place in this whole dream scenario. Could you tell me about your life with her?"

I was surprised at Olivia's leap into this past episode of my life, but I understood why she went there. There was a logic to Olivia's approach, an attempt to examine individual segments of this dream and help me to understand what significance each played in relation to the overall narrative. Together, we had already explored the perceived relation between the characters in the dream and the allegorical narrative that brought them to life. It did make sense to me at the time, but Olivia's aim was to better understand how these relationships in my life played out in real time.

So, my story began. Julia and her siblings were raised in an affluent neighborhood in North West London. Her father was a successful lawyer and partner in a law firm, and her mother was an interior decorator. Julia became a social worker before later finding her niche, working for a company in London that developed working strategies for burnt-out corporate types.

I lived with Julia Watts for almost a year, initially meeting her at a charity run shortly after my return to England. We dated for about three months, before Julia moved into my Greenwich apartment. Our relationship in the first year was solid, and could be best described as conventional and supportive. We had fun together, met with friends, went on dates, valued our private time, and took a vacation now and then when time would permit. Our sex life was good, and I always felt we were good friends. I was never sure how well I fit into the Watts family plan, but I seemed to be accepted by them, and we made our way through all obligatory family events without any noticeable problems or issues.

As our relationship moved on, I began to isolate myself on occasion, and I became emotionally detached—even though it wasn't a conscious decision at the time. The warning signs were there, but I found it easier to ignore or dismiss them, thinking it would come to pass and we would find our way back to the stability and common ground that characterized our relationship in the first year. Julia had a lot of friends, and I didn't have many, so it began to feel like I was living her life in many ways—focusing on what made her happy, while I simply sat back and accepted our life without protest. I was present and attentive to her, but I was drawing inward, losing myself amidst my wandering mind, floundering, much like somebody guiding or navigating a boat through a dense fog.

Eventually I could feel myself pulling away from Julia and she from me, from the normalcy that characterized our lives, and soon small disagreements became major points of contention. My sense of detachment heightened with each passing day, a chasm that widened and deepened, forcing us apart, and breaking the connectedness that held us together so effectively in the past. We did have our talks from time to time, but our lives became stagnant, and I lost my way—not knowing how, or even if, I wanted to re-energize our lives.

I found myself staying at work, avoiding home and the responsibilities of a relationship that existed back there, finding my solace in talking to colleagues instead of my partner, unable to find my way back. Flynn told me one day to make it right with Julia, and he did his best to encourage a return to my old life, and to regain the solidarity that had once characterized my life with this beautiful young woman. However, I was traveling on a different road than most, and I lost my way, with nothing at my disposal to guide me back. Julia was a lovely, caring individual, and I think in many ways I never felt worthy of her, and so I built my wall, devised an effective plan of self-sabotage, and eventually destroyed all that we had together.

It was easy to blame myself for most of it, and when life brought me to such a formidable crossroads as it did, the structure of my everyday life started to break down, and I found myself adrift, isolated, and without purpose. Julia and I existed together in the same residence, unable to engage in positive talk or bring a remedy to our damaged situation, and on a dismal Thursday evening in September, after a long day's work, I walked into our apartment which had been cleared of her belongings—she must have reached her limit.

I never had the chance to speak to Julia after that, exiled from her life without any hope of ever communicating with her. Eventually I began to piece together all those things which seemingly had been affecting me for quite some time—so many things that had come together to conspire against me. That was my take on it, but I was being the victim, unable to face or accept the fact that I had torn down that relationship, leaving it in ruins and forcing Julia to leave without saying goodbye. There was a strong desire on my part to explain all of this to Julia, apologize to her and tell her I was sorry for being so absent, but I was never given the opportunity.

I never phoned her, as I'd always held the belief that if somebody doesn't want you in their life, then why persist? Who would ever choose to be known as some pathetic victim pounding at their ex-girlfriend's parents' door, or stalking her outside her place of work? In the end, my inadequacies crept in and taunted me, reminding me that I wasn't worthy of a partner such as Julia in the first place—and I believed it. Her family protected her—communication was not permitted, and I was left with truly never knowing if it could have been saved. Our breakup was unsettling, simple, and uncomplicated, and my life went on. I worked, I ran, I ate, and I slept—but I was destroyed inside, desperately trying, and failing, to recoup my sense of self-worth and find satisfaction in the small pleasures of life again. That sense of self-blame and guilt for losing Julia remained within me, reminding me daily of my inability to take responsibility for making things right when it was within my power, and sadly, that part of my life had come to pass, gone, without any chance of revival.

Shortly after the demise of our relationship, I heard through a rather cruel, distant acquaintance that Julia had met someone at work—a manager type, fast track, square jaw, and very dashing. I missed her and all those times we had shared together, but I had truly become my own saboteur, the victim of my own undoing, and though maybe there were some things in my past that contributed to it all, I was the one who elected to stand still and let it all pass by. I was never disloyal to her, ever—yet I had removed myself from her life and never fought hard enough to win her back. I lay down my sword and accepted defeat, as I had so many other times in the past. It had become all about blaming myself for what had happened.

Olivia felt it all made sense—that in my dream narrative, I simply stood across from the family home and peered from a distance, removed from lives that were lost amidst the darkened landscape.

"In that dream, you're just an observer, dressed in black, hiding in the dark. Julia's departure brought you to your knees and you simply surrendered, and it was perfect, because then you could beat yourself up and carry around all that guilt and blame as you do. You know, I have an analogy for you—imagine you are carrying around a backpack every day full of bricks and rocks that weigh you down and hold you back. Eventually you become anesthetized to the damage that it's doing to your back and shoulders and whatever else. I'm not sure what's in that backpack of yours, but I think both you and I have a pretty good idea."

This was the only time in my relationship with Olivia that I excused myself, collected my belongings, and left without saying anything. I felt hurt by what she said—those sharpened arrows of truth had pierced me—and as I walked on, I remembered what Olivia had said to me in a previous session: "Mike, I think maybe you push people away, because you're afraid they're going to leave you, and you have lost the gift of connectedness and intimacy. You have few friends because you forgot how to share, how to bond, and it just becomes easy to walk away."

How right she was—walking away was always the easy thing to do.

I found my way to a small coffee shop along the way and sat looking out, feeling downtrodden and even angry at myself for not conducting myself in a more mature manner. Yet, I felt angry at Olivia for her rather brash, unsympathetic approach. She had torn down my defenses before, and now she was back, striking out at me when I least expected it. I hadn't felt this much anger and confusion in such a long time. I didn't know if I wanted to continue with counseling. How much easier it would be to pack it all in and return to my old life where the routine of my everyday existence, had kept me safe and apart from painful memories of the past. I was a mess and worst of all, I was alone, not wanting to speak to anybody, even entertaining the idea of leaving my job and life here in London and seeking out a new refuge where I could go back to asking all the questions and never having to answer any. It sounded good right about now.

Maybe there was value to being the observer, the anonymity of blending into the backdrop of life without others taking notice. I couldn't face sharing any of this with my mother or sister—partly out of shame, but mainly having to admit that the emotional repercussions of revisiting my painful past had suddenly turned my life upside down. I didn't know what to do, how to find relief from it all, or how to escape the frustration and anger that had found its way back to me.

I sat for about ten minutes before my phone ringing awakened my wandering mind, and upon answering I was surprised to hear Olivia's voice.

"Mike, why did you leave today?"

I wasn't sure why Olivia would ask such an obvious question, so I was eager to fill in the blanks as much as possible.

"Why do you think, Olivia? You tore me down about my father not so long ago, and now today…What the hell? I thought you'd be the last person to highlight my shortcomings and yeah, maybe I do beat myself up, but you know what, I don't need to be fucking reminded of it—especially by you. I'm broken. Is that what you need me to say? Maybe I'm too fucked up to face all my past mistakes? My father's dead, Julia's long gone, I cut my mom and sister out of my life for years, and to be honest, I really don't have a close friend to my name—so how do you expect me to feel good about any of this? You know what, I don't care what's in that backpack of mine that you described. I'm the one carrying it around, so I don't really care what you, or other people, think of the messiness that I lug around. Who cares anyway?"

There was a long silence on the other end of the phone, until she finally replied, "Look, what's done is done—we can't undo those moments in our lives. But we can begin to find our way back to a good place, and I was getting there with you, maybe a bit clumsily in retrospect, but then you decided you had enough today. Are you okay? I just wanted to make sure you're feeling okay. Will I see you next week?"

I wasn't sure what I wanted at this point. Why did it matter any longer? I was just a client to Olivia, nothing more. But she was right about one thing—what's done is done, and that's the tragedy of it all.

"I'm not sure if I'll be back. I thought this whole therapy thing was about feeling better. I'm just not feeling it."

"Okay. I understand how difficult recalling your relationship with Julia must have felt today, and a lot of emotions, thoughts, and feelings came out and got in the mix. And yeah, we explored the tragedy of your father and your separation from your family—and yes, it will feel unsettling. I do understand all of that."

I remained on the phone, not saying anything in response. I simply did not have the energy to think on it any longer.

"Mike, are you there?"

"Yeah, I'm here."

"One last thing. You're not broken. You've been stuck, and it's completely understandable considering all that you've been through. But you're getting there now. It may not feel like it, but you are. I'll let you go now. One more thing—despite this fallout as you see it, please remember to be kind to yourself."

As I sat and drank my coffee, I thought of Julia and truly hoped she was having a good life. I was sorry for what I had done, for my complete disconnect and abandonment of that relationship. But as I reminisced, Olivia's last words of advice about being kind to myself distracted me and forced me to stay in the present. I had dwelled too long on my mistakes and punished myself too many times for those past transgressions—and now maybe the time was right to take another step forward on that rickety bridge.

Following on from my rather unfortunate appointment with Olivia, I went on a four-day hiatus from life, hiding out in my apartment—the only exceptions being a visit to pick up groceries, my late evening runs, and a Sunday morning walk through Greenwich Park. I literally spoke to no one, even using the self-checkout at the supermarket to avoid any human interaction. I avoided the office too, choosing to work from home on Friday and Monday.

Friday had proved to be hit-and-miss, as my mind was distracted and I struggled to focus on my work assignments. However, I managed to see myself through until the end of the day, finally calling it quits at a rather late hour before heading out on my usual late-night run. I was struggling to bring any sense of resolve to the mix of emotions that were depriving me from finding balance in my life. I was reliving the phone conversation I had with Olivia and wondered what she must have thought of my mindset after our call ended. But what did it matter? I stayed up late that evening, watching reruns of alpine skiing events on some European sports channel. It proved to be oddly comforting. That night I had a restless sleep, and simply could not turn off my wandering mind—any effort to rid myself of negative, intrusive thoughts was not working.

When Saturday morning rolled around, I felt tired and lacking in the energy needed to get my day started. As a result, and despite a rather strong morning coffee, I ended up falling asleep on my sofa, only waking late in the morning thanks to a very loud motorcycle that unkindly roared down the street.

The remainder of Saturday was spent in front of my television watching YouTube videos, living a vicarious existence through the adventures and exploits of those who were seeking a greater meaning in their lives. After an unremarkable late dinner, I made an attempt to watch a comedy film, but it became clear there was nothing that was going to distract me or lighten my mood. So halfway through the film, I turned it off and went for a run, trying to find some outlet that would liberate me from the emotional tedium and confusion that was pulling me downward. As I ran, the anger that was resurrected because of my counseling session continued to swirl about, and I worried that maybe any effort to find solace or a sense of relief from it all might be out of reach. I couldn't decide whether to continue with counseling, or retreat to my safe place, where it would be easier to live a life of anonymity and detachment.

After ignoring repeated calls from Flynn on Sunday morning, I eased into the day by reading away most of the morning before making my way down to Greenwich Park for a leisurely stroll. I walked through the flower garden, before making my way out into the main part of the park. I eventually found a comfortable grassy spot and remained there for a long time, contemplating all that had happened since my unfortunate accident.

As I sat looking out, I experienced an incredible moment of clarity that helped me focus my thinking, and kindly brought a sense of rationality back to my runaway mind. It became clear to me that my anger with Olivia was simply misplaced, and blaming her and walking away had become the easy thing to do.

As I sat on that grassy slope looking outward, I realized that facing up to my painful life experiences was something that had to be done, so the process of healing could continue, and I could finally find my way back to life. I was sorry for what I had done, as Olivia was simply trying to guide me to a place where I could safely explore those painful memories within the confines of her office. But I didn't give her a chance. I finally understood that these sessions did not open old wounds—they simply exposed past wounds that had painfully remained open, never healing to begin with because of my own defiant refusal to look inward. I would return to her office on Thursday, this time with a better sense of understanding and a commitment to move forward with a renewed sense of confidence and self-belief.

Monday was the last day of my self-imposed hiatus. Over those four days, I spoke to no one, and instead languished for the first two days wallowing for the most part in self-pity and negative self-talk. However, this respite offered me the opportunity to choose— to either retreat to where I had started, or to continue moving forward, even though the healing journey was not without its challenging, arduous moments. By choosing the healing journey, I had made a commitment to keep myself in motion, and along the way, emptying that proverbial backpack of mine of any unwanted emotional baggage.

My hiatus had come to an end. A rather uneventful time in some respects, yet a period of self-reflection that allowed me the chance to rediscover my sense of courage against the battered backdrop of anger and self-doubt. Despite some trepidation, I was ready for what awaited me now, eager to regain my life balance and find my way back to the visible world.

13

There is nothing quite like a Michigan autumn. Crisp temperatures, blue skies for the most part, and the allure of the open road. Fall time in Michigan has a sense of character and liveliness about it, as the season generates a spectacular display of reds, yellows, and oranges, with the leaves transitioning from their familiar green into a panoramic blitz of color.

When I was young, we would pile into the family car every autumn and head up to the northlands of Michigan to visit family and pay tribute to Mother Nature as she shared this fall spectacular for all to see. We would all take turns raking the dried leaves at my aunt Jenny's house, dragging them along on a tarp to the big pile we had created at the far end of their large yard, and watch as my uncle Robert would set alight the remnants of a Michigan autumn.

I can remember standing and staring into the fire, almost mesmerized as the once-colorful leaves were quickly set ablaze, feeding the ongoing bonfire, all the while illuminating the nearby landscape with a magical, comforting light. Because our burning ritual was a post-dinner event, we would even have a few s'mores before Aunt Jenny would steal away the leftovers to ensure there were no sick stomachs to be had at the end of the evening.

We used to stand close to the fire until it was too hot to endure, and when we finally made it inside, our clothes and hair would carry the pleasant smell of smoke, as the remaining embers faded slowly into a gray and darkened ash pile outside. Eventually, Uncle Robert would fully extinguish the smoldering embers with the green garden hose that stood ready for action when called upon.

I was being beckoned back to this land now, a strong pull compelling me, calling out to me, and demanding my attention and presence. Maybe it was my session with Olivia resurrecting memories of my father and family, reminding me of those beautiful times when life felt so uncomplicated and pure. I needed to go to Michigan, to Honovi Lake on my own, to hopefully put my father's death to rest. I was realistic that the haunting memory of how my father died would live on, and I knew that I would continue at times to wrestle with the guilt and pain that had accompanied me for so very long, but I needed to face it all, and not hide any longer, or seek shelter behind the doors of a vacant life where I had sought refuge for so long. It was over, and what happened will always live on to some extent.

I was, however, seeking a way out, finding forgiveness for myself, relief and maybe even comfort by bringing myself back to the spot where my father sought that very same comfort when he visited his small hometown on so many occasions. I didn't want that lake to remain a place of unresolved grief. It was a beautiful spot, and I wanted it to remind me of all those cherished moments when I visited there as a young child with my father, sitting on the banks of the lake amongst the grasses and wildflowers, appreciating the calm and serenity of the moment as we stared out at the beauty of it all.

I flew to Detroit, stayed in a nearby airport hotel, arose early the next morning, and completed the very long five-hundred-mile journey in just under nine hours, only stopping along the way to eat and get fuel. I told nobody of my plans, other than Jon Finney, who proved very understanding. I had originally thought about sharing my plans with my mother and sister, but knew it would turn into more of a production than I was ready for. So, as much as it pained me, I kept my travel plans to myself. There are some journeys in life that we must undertake on our own, and this was one of them.

The small roadside motel that I stayed in was located about twenty miles from Westfield, as I was hoping to maintain my anonymity, unnoticed by any long-term residents in the area. I found myself drawn to this area for other reasons, as traditional folklore about the elusive Bigfoot was prevalent throughout the area. There were local businesses, shops, and even books on the subject scattered around this part of Michigan, and oddly enough, as I dined alone in a small café that evening, I found myself in conversation with two older gentlemen, Oscar and Archie, sitting across from me, who regularly went on excursions seeking out Bigfoot, in the western woodlands of Upper Michigan. Their absolute belief in something that appeared more of tall tales than anything of actual credibility piqued my curiosity, and left me in awe of their unwavering belief in this woodland's phenomena.

The next morning greeted me with a clear sky and crisp temperatures. After buying a coffee to go, a morning muffin, and a copy of the local *Western Gazette*, I headed out to Honovi Lake, and once parked up, ventured out through the woods, making my way down a very well-groomed trail, reaching the lake in about fifteen minutes. I walked to a rather flat and shaded spot, providing me with a nice view of the lake and surrounding area. Honovi Lake seemed peaceful, and as I leaned against a welcoming maple tree, I stared out and was grateful for the morning calm.

Looking out upon the lake, I thought of my father, the man that he was, the love he had for his family, for the positive commitment he made to this world, and for his deep respect and passion for nature.

As I stood and thought of my father, questions that had repeated themselves to me so often returned to me yet again: *Why did you go to that conference, why did you go for that early morning walk, why did you die on that day, why did this happen to you, to us, why? Why didn't I go with you to that conference, why didn't I walk with you on that fateful morning, why wasn't I with you, why did I abandon you, why did I leave you alone on that day, why?*

There were a hundred questions that pounded at me relentlessly, but I realized they could not be easily answered. Oddly, as disconcerting as my counseling session had been with Olivia when we talked about my father's death, it had somehow offered me this opportunity to face it all, acknowledge my pain, and make an effort to make peace with myself.

I stood for a while longer and looked out at the lake, until such time that I felt a sense of calm and relief wash over me. I knew this process would not end with this journey, yet it was a start, a way of facing all that I had avoided for so long. Further along, a large, flat elevated rock offered me a sunny seat overlooking the lake, providing me comfort and the opportunity to sit and reflect further upon times past when we would visit this area of Michigan, walking through the woodlands surrounding the lake before finding our own place to sit and appreciate those moments together.

As I began to make my way out, I came upon a couple wearing matching green backpacks and each carrying a walking stick. The two hikers greeted me as though we were long-lost friends. They were in their sixties, I guessed, suited up and ready for what appeared to be a rather vigorous walk through the woodlands. After we exchanged pleasantries, I was told that the forest service had put in some new walking trails in the area, and that it might be worth my while to have a look around.

Before we parted ways, the gentleman moved closer to me and offered me a bit of happy day advice, with a sense of genuine encouragement in his voice, "You know, it's fantastic out here in all this nature. So, enjoy your walk, because today is going to be a beautiful day."

I felt grateful to this man, who took the time to reach out to this lost soul, offering me a small bit of encouragement to seek out those stopping points in life that would provide me with both comfort and meaning.

Once in the car I skimmed through the *Western Gazette* I had picked up, taking special notice of job advertisements in the local area. One rather prominent ad caught my attention. A cultural and historical center located in the small community of Redfern was seeking out a marketing and communications professional, in part to promote enterprises and opportunities around learning and education, arts, media, and Indigenous studies and related projects.

Redfern is a small community or town of about 1500 people located in the Keweenaw Peninsula of Upper Michigan, a place where my father took us on several occasions during our regular visits back to his homeland. The Keweenaw Peninsula is the northernmost part of Michigan, a beautiful swatch of land that juts out into the cold waters of Lake Superior. The Keweenaw Peninsula is a distinctive geographical feature that helps characterize the overall unique shape of Michigan. Any sharp-eyed map enthusiast can easily locate Michigan's two unique peninsulas, as they are nestled in and surrounded by the mighty Great Lakes.

My father liked Redfern. This small town was much like what one would expect when traveling through on their way to the northern tip of Michigan. A small main street, dotted with local stores, eateries, coffee shops, bars—and even a couple of very cool antique and collectible shops. I always liked driving to Redfern with my parents. It was an adventure into small-town America, where most people knew each other and the air seemed so clean and refreshing, offering you an opportunity to breathe again, to value something that is so obviously absent in big city life. Like many Upper Michigan towns, it had character and a mystery about it that lured you in and kept you captivated.

During the Michigan autumn, Redfern would become aglow with vibrant color, a feast for all those who ventured to it. However, Redfern and this entire area of Michigan were beset with brutal, unforgiving winters. Record snowfalls and frigid temperatures often left the area marred with icy roads, limiting travel, and forcing even the strongest of hearts to find shelter and comfort within the confines of their heated homes, away from the brutal assault that could prove relentless and unmerciful. I had witnessed this onslaught on many an occasion, all part of the experience, the whole adventure of living in the northlands of the United States.

Upon leaving Honovi Lake and Westfield, with the best intentions of heading eastward, my journey came to a sudden stop at a very familiar fork in the road that I remembered so well. Without much time to consider my options, I soon made the impulsive decision to drive northward up into the Keweenaw Peninsula, seeking out the small town of Redfern.

Once in Redfern, I made my way to the two-story Michigan State Historical Center, which houses the Cultural Center and upper-floor library. It was an incredible building to visit, constructed in the 1890s, and characterized by its Renaissance Revival design. Once inside, one is greeted with a modernized lower floor, accommodating offices, and a variety of displays—including a historical overview of both the local area and the state. A small canteen rests at the far end of the main floor, offering all who visit a chance to sit and soak in the unique ambiance of this building. Visitors can take an elevator or a grand staircase to the second-floor library overlooking the main floor on all four sides, with beautiful wooden railings enclosing the upper floor, and stacks upon stacks of books resting upon antique wooden shelves.

Upon completion of my leisurely tour, I headed over to a small greeting area where I was handed a detailed description of the marketing and communications position as per my request. As I stood and scanned through the details, I was approached by a man who introduced himself as Adam Clifton, the manager of the center, who took notice of my interest in the job advert. Adam, who appeared to be in his late thirties, was quite tall, had a warm face, light brown or almost blond hair cut quite short, and was casually dressed. He exuded a natural warmth and was quick to explain that the center had recently received a joint state and federal grant, with plans to build an annex outside and expand learning and cultural services throughout the entire area. He explained that he and his Norwegian wife Linnea were responsible for running the center, and were excited by the long-term development plans that had been carefully orchestrated over the past year.

After briefly introducing myself and explaining what I did for a living, indicating I was looking to move away from city life and seek out a career change, Adam was eager to hear more. Without sharing any personal history, I told Adam I had a strong desire to move back to the States, preferably to a town such as Redfern, where I could enjoy the outdoors and a much slower pace of life. Adam was quick to respond to my interest in the position and said there was plenty of time for me to consider applying for the role.

"Of course," he stated, "there would be formal interviews and such, but you sound like you'd be a great fit."

We talked for some time before exchanging emails and phone numbers, as Adam encouraged me to contact him personally if I had any questions once I had returned to London.

I had made a previous reservation at a small local hotel, and before I headed out, Adam presented me with a book written by a local historian, highlighting the history of the area, including key geographical information, as well as local demographics, evolution of local communities, and even an overview of the Historical and Cultural Centers. The book contained photos, anecdotal episodes from community members, and a fascinating perspective of the Keweenaw Peninsula.

Once back in my hotel room, I thumbed through the book, captivated by some of the old photos, including the Cultural Center from times past. It was indeed interesting and thought-provoking, and I finally set it aside, promising myself to have a thorough read on my plane journey back to the UK.

In the morning, and after a restful night's sleep, I had a walk around town, stopped in at a local restaurant called The Peppercorn for breakfast, before putting on my running attire and enjoying a pleasant, steady jog around the area. It was uplifting running through such a quiet and charming landscape, remembering along the way times past when my sister and I would walk alongside our parents, navigating some of these very same streets and scenic paths. My father loved Upper Michigan—it was his true home, a place where he had the freedom to enjoy the pleasures of the outdoors as we hiked through woodlands, fished, and took what seemed like endless photographs of nature and colorful landscapes, and any wildlife that might cross his path. We would often venture to the shores of Lake Superior, where we would sit and listen, witnessing the power of nature as the unbridled waves of this mighty Great Lake would pound relentlessly upon the rocky shoreline.

As I grew older, I came to realize that my father never really fit with our Chicago life, as acknowledged by my mother, who once told me that when they relocated to Chicago, my father sadly lost his connection with his Michigan life that once brought him so much purpose and value. Despite making a life in Chicago and raising a family, he would only really come alive when they returned to their homeland, and he could once again connect with the land, the people, and the rugged nature that he held in such reverence.

My flight back to England was a pleasurable one. I settled in and for the first time in a very long while, I felt a sense of lightness about me, difficult to define in some respects, but it was soothing and reassuring. Gazing out the window of the plane, I thought of my father and smiled, remembering all those beautiful moments we shared together throughout our lives. This brief trip back to Michigan rekindled those dormant memories, and I could see him so clearly, walking with me in the woodlands of Michigan, smiling at me along the way, telling me stories of his own childhood, while teaching me to appreciate the wonders of nature and, best of all, just living in the moment.

As the two of us walked through fallen leaves, my father would tell me to remain quiet and listen to the silent stories that the beautiful woodlands were telling us. Those memories, those moments had now returned to me, awakened once again from such a lengthy slumber. I found it fascinating that so many of the memories were those very times in Michigan when we returned to my parents' homeland to visit family and walk amongst nature and the beauty of it all. Maybe, because I became such a city boy growing up in Chicago, these woodland experiences became so burned into my memory, triggering this desire to lose myself in the mysticism and wonder of this incredible land.

I put my head back, hoping to get a bit of sleep before digging into the book that Adam kindly presented to me. However, my intrusive daydreaming would not afford me that pleasure and sleep would have to wait, as my mind played out all kinds of thoughts, scenarios, and fantasies. I once read that our minds wander about forty-seven percent of the time. Personally, I believe myself to be at a much higher percentage than the average person. Not exactly a Walter Mitty type, but not too far off.

My mind-surfing experience led me down the path to my experience in Redfern. I don't think I truly appreciated just how meaningful my encounter with Adam had been—a possibility in the form of a job, to step away from my life, to break away from an existence and career that had kept me safe, avoiding any kind of risk, hiding in London amongst the big city and all its distractions. Working in some small town, fraternizing with the locals, and leading a life in complete contrast to my current situation…could that work?

I owed it to myself to look inward, to begin to understand how new opportunities could change my life for the better, and while living in a small town in Michigan may or may not be the place for me, it was all about keeping an open mind and thinking of new possibilities. I sat for some time, thinking of what life might be like living in this small town, becoming immersed in the outdoors, finding my place and purpose in a life devoted to seeking solace, while moving at a slower pace, with less stress, living with more definition and meaning. The complete opposite to my life in London—how tempting it all felt, to leave that noise and chaos behind. I savored the idea of walking through the woodlands, along scenic lakeshores, or traversing the roads of small-time living—compared to navigating the busy roads of London, hurrying to scheduled appointments, while stressing out about looming deadlines. The answer seemed clear. I wasn't finding what I needed living in London any longer, and maybe destiny was calling out to me—time to move on and seek out and discover where it was I really belonged.

A couple of years ago I met a freelance writer by the name of

Brennan Brewer, who proved to be one of the most interesting people I had ever come upon. I met Brennan at a media conference in London, where he was visiting from Canada. Brennan and I agreed to a pub lunch, as I was interested in hearing his take on going fully freelance. Eventually the conversation shifted gears to the personal side of things.

Brennan had previously led what he had described as a very conventional, humdrum life. He grew up near Brussels, raised by conservative parents—he went to school, attended university, and ended up in a rather dissatisfying marketing job with an international company in the heart of his home city. He met a woman at work and found himself going through the motions of a relationship, yet one that eventually became devoid of any emotional connection. His desire to become a writer seemed nothing more than a distant and diminishing dream, and he found himself dissatisfied with his work, feeling he was no longer compatible with his career nor his colleagues. His life, as he had told me, just simply got stuck in one place and he found himself going through the motions with no way out. He got involved in an unrewarding relationship with a woman, and remained there, because much like his job, he became lazy and didn't have the courage to find his way out of things.

However, during a work trip to the Canadian province of Ontario, Brennan found himself drawn to the spirit of Canada, the call of the outdoors, and the romantic vision of living in a small cabin somewhere in the middle of nowhere. Upon his return to Brussels, Brennan never discussed his feelings with anyone, including his girlfriend or parents, who all would have dismissed his idea of a life in the wilds of Canada as being a flight of fancy. So, he kept it all to himself. Returning to Canada for work sometime later, Brennan was again beset by feelings of discord about his life back in Belgium, yet was unable to find the courage to change his life and so remained unsettled—struggling with a job he no longer had any connection with, and a difficult relationship with a girlfriend who seemed miles away from him.

One rainy day, after attending a wedding with his parents and girlfriend, Brennan went for an evening walk on his own and experienced, as he described to me, 'a profound catharsis'—and with that, a decision was made that would change his life forever. After some research and preparation, Brennan resigned from his job, liquidated his financial assets, and made the decision to move to Canada. The process was quick, yet not without its pain and sorrow. Brennan left behind a girlfriend, family, and friends, offering no one any reason or clue as to why he made this choice.

Brennan told me outright that at the time it was indeed an act of desperation—an escape from all that he knew, all that was keeping him anchored in a place he no longer wanted to be. Brennan left home and moved to Canada and found solace in a small northern Ontario village. He turned to freelance writing, met an incredible woman named Eva—a kindred spirit in just about all things—and married her one fine day about a year later. Brennan said he found his ideal life with a woman who shared his zest for a simple, but meaningful and purposeful life.

"It made sense," he told me. "It was all so uncomplicated."

That was his story in a nutshell.

As I sat back, my thoughts remained on Brennan and his decision to abandon his life. Maybe there was a lack of courage there—maybe Brennan took the easy way out of it all, and subsequently sneaking out the back door in some respects seemed like the right choice at the time, despite the consequences that followed. All I knew in the end was that Brennan had found his place—he was happy there, living the life he had long desired.

Remembering this encounter, I had to ask myself if I was any different than Brennan Brewer. My own situation was certainly not dissimilar to his. Maybe my move to London was a way to escape like Brennan had done, only packaged a bit differently. Yet I didn't escape to some quiet and quaint setting—instead moving from one big city to another, losing myself again in the melee and noise of the madding crowd.

So, what to do? What would it be like to pack your bag, buy a one-way ticket, leave your current life behind, and simply walk out the door, travel to a new destination, and establish a new life? Yet, I had done it once before—different circumstances, different results—and I could more than likely do it again. I could buy that ticket, leave with no regrets, and find a new life, probably back in the States, finding my way to a small town where I could live a life free of all the noise and chaos that had surrounded me for so very long.

Or would I simply be running again, instead of looking inside and trying to understand what was motivating me to want to leave?

I'm not sure what Brennan Brewer felt inside, or what type of person he was, or what it was that spurred him on to make such a big life change. Why hadn't he shared his thoughts and feelings with his girlfriend in a more forthright manner? Would there have been a better outcome for the two of them? From what Brennan told me, no one, including his girlfriend, would understand what he truly desired out of life. Maybe he was an adult runaway in some respects, or maybe he was simply searching for something to help him find his way to that place where life finally made sense.

I felt Brennan's choice in the end was a selfish one, and his decision to leave without any attempt to remedy his relationship with his partner was dishonorable. I didn't want to be that person who lacked the courage to do the right thing, instead opting for a quick escape. In many regards I had chased Julia out of my life, unable to find the courage to find my way out of that dark place where I had existed for so long. I had no right to judge Brennan for his actions—yet I no longer wanted to be the person I used to be, hiding away, unable to discover intimacy, while figuratively running away from the responsibilities of life.

My meandering mind finally came to and stopped upon my quirky encounter with Oscar and Archie, the two true believers, who ramble their way through the woodlands of Upper Michigan in search of the legendary Bigfoot. How fascinating these two were. As I replayed their tales of the elusive Bigfoot, and hearing the conviction in their voices, I smiled—not dismissively, but instead in appreciation for their attitude and determination to carry on with their mission to seek out this legendary creature, regardless of the naysayers.

Despite meeting so many interesting and larger-than-life characters in London, this experience in Michigan stood out to me—reminding me that very often we can all find meaning and purpose in our lives if we are willing to take the risk and open our world up to those people we meet along the way.

Perhaps more than anything, Oscar and Archie reminded me that life moves on, even after tragic events happen—the world keeps moving. This odd blend of my father's memories, intermingled with a brief encounter with two fascinating men in western Upper Michigan, spoke to me about the constant ebb and flow of life, and the importance of not losing sight of a life to be lived. I couldn't undo what happened to my father, yet I could reintegrate myself back into the mainstream of life. My father was gone, his ashes scattered over a beautiful and natural landscape, and despite my best efforts to isolate myself, circumstances prevailed and led me down a path of discovery and an opportunity to simply live again. Perhaps my meeting with Oscar and Archie, along with visiting Honovi Lake, had proven to be life-affirming, and prompted me to appreciate the value of living a meaningful life without regret.

My journey to Michigan came to an end, saying goodbye to my father again while gazing out at Honovi Lake, and possibly discovering a stopping point that had offered me a long-awaited sense of solace.

14

It was a Saturday morning in October when Flynn came knocking at my door. We had agreed to meet at my place, have a morning run together, and then head over to his house for a late breakfast with Emily. There was a chill in the air, but the day rewarded us with blue skies and just a slight breeze as we headed out towards Greenwich Park. Our running pace was comfortable, relaxing more than anything, as was often typical of our runs together, since we generally spent the time together chatting about anything and everything.

Earlier, I had told Flynn about my impromptu trip back to Michigan, and my visit to Redfern to check on the job at the Historical and Cultural Center. Flynn remained silent as I told him of my conversation with Adam Clifton, yet I wanted some feedback, curious as to what his thoughts might be about my changing my life, leaving the big city, and seeking out a new beginning. Flynn remained reticent, other than the occasional exclamation of surprise as I continued to explain my motives for possibly exploring a complete change of scenery.

When we finally finished our leisurely jog around the park, we treated ourselves to coffee and found a sunny spot in the open meadow area to sit and talk further. Flynn was indeed curious, but I sensed he was a bit hesitant in what he said to me, more than likely not wanting to be dismissive of my idea.

"Wow, that's fascinating. I mean, how would you feel living in such a small town and all?"

"I don't know exactly. I mean, I just feel like I'm stuck living here, and I don't know, I like my job and all, but there's times I just want something different for myself. Who knows, I think maybe—good things come to those who take risks. I don't know, there are so many thoughts passing through my mind."

Flynn looked over at me with a rather perplexed look on his face.

"Well, you know what's best for yourself. But if you're thinking of becoming freelance and all, why accept a job over there if you're thinking of changing gears completely? I mean, why wait to go freelance and why move if your career choices are under consideration?"

I could appreciate what Flynn was saying, as my own motives for moving weren't even that clear to me. I wasn't sure if it was the prospect of a job opportunity, or if I was simply enticed by my father's homeland and my subsequent desire to seek a life defined more by solitude.

"Dude, have you told anybody else, I mean your family or anybody else?"

"No, I think maybe I need to sort this one out on my own. It's been helpful sharing it with you, though. Appreciate your thoughts on the matter, as brief as they were."

Flynn laughed at my retort.

"Dude, we've been friends for a very long time. You are one of the closest friends I have outside of Emily. When you moved back here, well, I celebrated that moment. I mean, we saw each other over the years, but when you came back, it was nice—and I'm not going to lie to you, it's been great being with my old friend again. But saying that, I want the best for you, no matter where that might be. So, I don't want to be one of those people who says the wrong thing and ends up raining on your parade. This is your life, and the only bit of advice I can offer is to really think it over before you make any major decisions."

I appreciated Flynn's advice. I had to get back to Adam at some point soon, but wanted to give myself a bit more time to think it all over. Flynn's few words of wisdom were valued, however, as it helped me to better understand that maybe my interest in the job and living in that quaint small town in Michigan was possibly just a pipe-dream.

Flynn looked over at me with a grin on his face.

"Dude, we best get going before Emily sends out a search party. Who knows, she might even contact you to ask for support, just like in your dream quest."

Before we started on our way back to his house, Flynn took the opportunity to ask me about my search for Sophie.

"I think my investigative skills are seriously lacking. I don't know anymore. I can't keep chasing a shadow—I've got a life to live and I'm doing my best to push this aside as much as possible. I think about her a lot, but who knows? Maybe she isn't out there. Maybe it's time to pack it all in."

Flynn's reply was spoken like a true friend.

"Listen, I think if there's a chance this woman is out there, and she's left this impression upon you, well I'd keep the search going at all costs. I mean, fair enough, I wouldn't let it dominate my life by any means, but who knows, you must have seen her somewhere to remember such a fine-looking woman."

My Thursday appointment with Olivia seemed quite timely, considering my recent trip to Michigan and my indifference about my career path and life in London. After my conversation with Flynn, and listening to his wise words, I wasn't sure if uprooting myself and moving back over to the States was such a wise choice—and despite my previous reluctance, I decided to share the details of my time in Michigan with Olivia, feeling she would be the one person who could help me gain a better understanding of it all.

Olivia listened as I spoke about the very emotional journey back to Honovi Lake and about my encounter with Adam Clifton, and the prospect of a possible career change.

There were a few moments of silence before she replied, "Well, sometimes making a choice based solely on an emotive response isn't always a bad thing. Saying that, however, your emotional journey has been more about trying to separate yourself from that young man back in Chicago who was so racked with guilt and grief, because he lived with the painful thought that he had abandoned his father. There is that possibility that you moved back to England when you had the chance, possibly trying to leave that behind. So, sometimes those emotive experiences can also mislead us and coerce us down the wrong path. Does that make sense?"

I felt confused by her response.

"I hear you, but my current situation is a bit different than before…"

Olivia took a deep breath before she spoke.

"A person doesn't need to move halfway across the world to become the person they want to be, or necessarily live the life they want to—or in your case, seek some type of absolution. That isn't necessary. I think you can change your life wherever you're at, and you don't need to reinvent yourself in the process. I can't answer those big questions. Maybe life in Michigan in that small town would be fantastic, but maybe finding self-acceptance and discovering meaningful connections might be a better first step."

As I walked away from Olivia's office, I experienced an incredible sense of enlightenment. Tonight, I would write to Adam Clifton and thank him for taking the time to speak to me about the job, but tell him I would be staying in London. My life here wasn't over and would continue until such a time when all the pieces would fall into place, and I was ready to seek out new destinations and new opportunities.

That evening, when I looked in the mirror before I headed off to bed, I appreciated that person a little more and recognized that, despite a few shortcomings, he wasn't so bad after all.

ON FRIDAY, I ARRIVED home after work feeling washed out, after spending most of the day with my head stuck in my laptop, trying to piece together some rather uninspiring historical narrative. Throughout the day I felt on edge, and a sense of angst and frustration pecked away at me—any effort on my part to dismiss or ignore it only seemed to heighten its impact on me. Struggling to keep focused, I took a brief afternoon stroll and allowed myself a strong coffee, hoping a caffeine fix might enliven my dampened mood.

Once home, I put some music on and sat back on the sofa for a while, hoping this brief respite would elevate my spirit. However, as I sat trying to live in the moment, I began to feel downtrodden and out of sorts, unable to process what was going on. Olivia did warn me that I might experience these moments during the counseling process, and not to consider them a setback.

After eating dinner, I sat and watched a twenty-four-hour news channel, which didn't particularly help my mood, so I considered a run, but despite my best intentions, the mind and body were just not willing. So, I sat back again on the sofa, listened to the music, hoping to distract myself from whatever it was that had invaded my headspace, and attempted to reframe my thinking by focusing on something positive—but nothing was working. A deep sense of melancholy had come to pay me a visit and with it, thoughts of my father raced through my mind, along with the mistakes of my broken relationship with Julia. Every self-doubt I had ever entertained about myself crept back in and subsequent feelings of loneliness and emptiness raised their heads, brutally tearing at my self-esteem and robbing me of my self-worth. How could this happen so quickly?

After sitting for some time and yielding to this torrent of emotion and subsequent self-pity, I finally managed to motivate myself and headed out for a run, despite the lateness of the hour. Running at a slower pace than usual, I was finally able to bring some clarity to it all, and attributed that unwelcomed relentless attack upon my self-esteem in part to my work with Olivia, as so much had resurrected from the past over the last couple of months. Facing both the loss of my father and Julia had left me broken and seemingly incapable of bringing any sense of resolve or forgiveness for my mistakes and misgivings.

However, on this evening, I was determined to find my way out, rediscover my lost life, and make amends for taking refuge in a lonely, tedious life.

IT WAS MY MOTHER'S birthday on October 21st and I had made plans to phone her early evening my time so we could have a proper chat together. After my father's death, my sister and family moved back to Ravenswood to live with my mother. It was the family home, and my mother—being undecided about what to do with it after my father was gone—had agreed that after some remodeling, living together with my sister and family seemed like the best option.

My mother had her own upstairs apartment, complete with living quarters, while Robyn, Peter, and the kids had the rest of the house.

After wishing her happy birthday, she informed me she was having dinner out that evening with Robyn and the family and my mother's sister Meg, who came to stay with her for a week.

"I got your beautiful bouquet of flowers, and the chocolates and champagne. A card would have been fine. Thank you so much."

I had to smile—every birthday conversation we'd ever had began with a similar pseudo-scolding, despite her reveling in the fact that her son made the effort to send her such thoughtful gifts.

"Mom, I also bought you some books, including a big garden book that I think you'll like. I sent them about five days ago, so I am assuming they haven't arrived."

"No, they haven't come yet. But that's so thoughtful of you."

"By the way, did you and Aunt Meg down your champagne yet?"

My mom laughed and laughed and then called out to her sister, "Meg, Michael was wondering if we emptied the bottle of champagne yet?"

Suddenly, without warning, my aunt Meg took over phone duties.

"Michael, hello my dear. No, we haven't touched it yet. We might even bring it to the restaurant this evening, or your mother and I might have a couple of glasses before we head out. Who knows?"

With that, I could hear them both share a laugh. After saying goodbye to my aunt, my mom returned.

"Michael, how are you doing? Are you looking after yourself?"

It was my mother's birthday, and I wasn't allowing her to switch the focus of our conversation, so I simply told her all was okay.

"Look, it's your birthday, so go out and enjoy yourself. I'll call in a few days to see how everything went."

After saying our goodbyes, I sat for a while thinking of my mom. I missed her a lot, and the family, and felt a passing moment of sadness, wishing I could be with them all.

I thought of the large garden book that I had sent along to my mom and Robyn, hoping they would find it useful. Oddly enough, as often happens with thought association, I soon found myself thinking of Sophie's snapdragons. I opened my laptop and began to enter Sophie's name into Google, but stopped suddenly and stared at the screen, undecided whether to proceed or to just leave it. How many late evenings had I wasted on this search? The answers simply weren't there.

I closed the laptop down, grabbed my notebook with my dream notes in it, and read about meeting Sophie in Garibaldi Square. It made it all feel alive again, feeding my wandering mind with pleasant images and the remembrance of a mysterious soul who reached out to me in a time of need. So interesting, that this memory remains so alive, so vivid, and returns me back to my dream when I sat with this beautiful woman, talked about flowers, and stared into her lovely eyes.

Goodnight Sophie. Thank you for those beautiful memories.

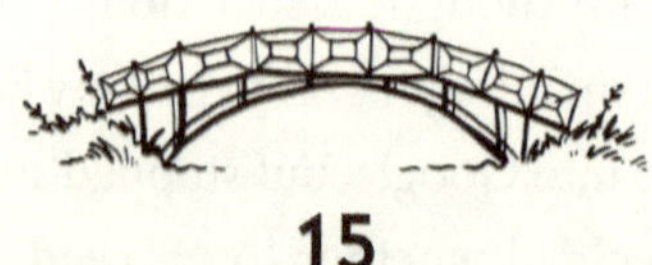

15

Spontaneity and my impulsive nature were at work once again, steering me ever so forcefully back to Nice. Sophie was never far from my thoughts, and scrolling through my blue journal filled with vivid descriptions of my experiences and encounters within my dream state, only served to further fuel my wild obsession.

Without much forethought or consideration, I arranged for a three-night stay in a seafront hotel along the Promenade des Anglais. Obsession or not, it was something I had to do—I believed Sophie was out there, somewhere waiting to be found, and I was convinced beyond a doubt she was living in Nice. Our lives must have intersected at some point in this city, so I had to continue the search and indulge my desire to find this woman, if she really existed.

During one of my sessions with Olivia, she shared an interesting perspective that I'd quickly dismissed afterward. Despite my insistence that Sophie was somewhere in Nice, Olivia was not convinced, and felt that my fixation on Nice may serve as a distraction or misdirection, a red herring of sorts, which might limit my ability to access other relevant information or other possible scenarios. At one point she even said to me, "You have kept yourself anchored to France this whole time, because you saw it in a dream, but just maybe you've been looking in all the wrong places, and as you well know, dreams aren't always what they appear to be."

Yet I was more than convinced that Sophie was there, strolling through Nice with flowers in hand, visiting the market stalls as she made her way to the nearest café. Sophie was there, and I was determined to find her.

As with my previous trip to Nice, I told no one and had no plan of action, other than occupying my familiar lookout posts, hoping to see this woman against the backdrop of this southern France city. I had done some research on municipal and governmental buildings in Nice, but most appeared to be off-limits and my lack of French would only frustrate potential inquiries. This search for Sophie seemed frivolous, much like my previous trip, and maybe it was all a waste of my time, but I had convinced myself there was method to my madness—and besides, a short break in the south of France was never a bad option. This time, however, I went as a true believer with all intention of finding her, never doubting my reasons or motives for making this journey.

I arrived early Friday morning in Nice, left my bag at the hotel and was soon out on the streets, strolling ever so slowly, taking in the sights and sounds of this seaside city. My eyes relentlessly studied the faces of all who passed by my line of sight, ensuring that no person went unnoticed. After my initial wandering, I began walking at a heightened pace, paying a visit to the Promenade des Anglais and Garibaldi Square, traversing the small lanes of the old town and eventually making my way to the Cours Saleya market. There was a determination about me, a one-man search party, diligent in my mission, hoping to visit and revisit key areas of the city, eager to see that one familiar face, allowing me the opportunity to say hello and to finally bring closure to this baffling mystery.

During my flight over, I had considered widening my search area, however I quickly abandoned this idea, knowing it would be unwise simply because it would be too much territory to cover—Nice was where we came together in my dream, meeting at Garibaldi Square and wandering through the market along Cours Saleya.

I walked back down the old town lanes to Garibaldi Square, and again sat in the very spot I had on my last visit, waiting patiently with the hope that a certain young woman would come walking my way. The young woman who waited on me and delivered my coffee and croissant spoke English, so I took the liberty of asking her if Antoine was working, and was informed that he was away on a short vacation and not back at work until early next week. So, like last time, I sat with a sense of anticipation, scanning the area and peering out at anybody who came walking along.

As soon as I finished my coffee, it was back to my familiar loop of traveling the old lanes down to the promenade and back to Cours Saleya, strolling along the many market stalls. The day proved uneventful, and as an early evening chill began to set in, I made my way to one of the many restaurants along Cours Saleya, sitting at one of the outdoor tables kept warm by an overhead heater and large plastic enclosure, enjoying a large plate of lasagna as I looked outward at everyone who passed by.

The next day was much the same—visiting Garibaldi Square in the morning, having a coffee and pastry, and then continuing the loop once again, walking familiar lanes and sitting along the seaside. However, I was beginning to feel an odd sense of disconnection, wandering alone, and wondering what this experience was all about. A sense of frustration had firmly set in, and my search was proving fruitless—a reminder that this indulgence of fantasy would end up leaving me more downtrodden than before. Unlike my previous visit to Nice, and despite my best intentions to maintain a positive mindset, I was beginning to struggle, and walking the streets of this city alone was wearing me down. Yet despite this sense of despair, and having had little expectation of success, my heart pounded with anticipation whenever I saw someone that even loosely resembled Sophie—and so the search continued.

On the morning of my last full day, I headed back out to Garibaldi Square, sat with coffee in hand and, after pondering my situation, decided to end my search. It had become a pointless exercise, wandering around this small corner of Nice, searching for someone who possibly did not even exist. It made no sense. After returning to my room, I grabbed my book, sat in the small hotel courtyard, and read the afternoon away. I was defeated, tired, and wanted to go home.

That evening, I walked along Cours Saleya searching for a place to eat, and upon reaching the far end of the street, towards the port side, I noticed a group of young men and women sitting at a table just outside the front of a restaurant having drinks. A young, dark-haired woman sitting amongst this group caught my attention and, just for a moment, my heart pounded with anticipation, as from afar there seemed a sense of familiarity about her. It seemed unlikely, yet a feeling of desperation was prodding at me, edging me onward, and without further hesitation I walked over and seated myself at a small table directly across from them, giving me a clear view of the young woman in question. But it was to no avail—I soon realized that nothing about this woman was familiar, and like my previous attempts at discovery, my hopes of randomly finding a mystery woman on the streets of Nice appeared only as a futile indulgence. I finished the drink I had ordered, sat for a while, and listened to the chatter that filled the cool evening air, and decided then that my search was truly over.

As I sat in my room that evening, I reflected upon my stay in Nice and wondered if I had learned anything from this mission, or was it just a sad attempt on my part to feed an obsession that was leading me astray, away from matters of the real world?

That night I lay on my bed and replayed the dream scenario in my mind, hoping that something would come alive, and all would be revealed. My mind churned over the details of the dream over and over, but without any answers forthcoming, I decided it was time to throw down my sword once again and leave this crusade behind. I had done my best, diligently undertaking my search, and yet it hadn't yielded any answers, and now I was out of solutions, ideas, and reasons to carry on.

It was time to get back to real life, once again.

My flight departed the next day around noon and as I sat back in my seat, I made myself a promise to leave it all behind and get on with living. That evening, I headed out for a run, traversing my familiar neighborhood streets, pushing myself until I reached the point of exhaustion, doing my best to shut off my wandering mind and accept that I had done my best to unravel this mystery.

ELIZABETH ADELAIDE WARNER CAME into this world on November 5th, a bit earlier than expected, weighing in at six pounds eight ounces. Flynn phoned with the good news, expressing the gratitude he felt for having witnessed this miracle of childbirth.

"She was born healthy," his shaky voice stated, "and that's all that matters to us."

In many ways, the birth of Lizzy, as she was quickly dubbed by Flynn, was a bit of a wake-up call for me. Lizzy's birth was yet another reminder to me that life does move on around us, and we may try and stay in that one place because it is comfortable, safe or what we know best, but maybe that isn't what life was designed to be like.

I wasn't worried about losing Flynn as a friend, but I knew that life would be different for him now, in a good way, and I wanted to be there with him to celebrate that whenever possible. Those are the meaningful and impactful moments in life, when we can support others and help celebrate their successes, achievements, and significant life events. Flynn and Emily were now parents, and I eagerly awaited the opportunity to congratulate them as they began an exciting and life-changing chapter in their lives.

After our call ended, I thought of Flynn and his place in my wandering dream. I realized that Flynn never ran from anything in his life—maybe, in that crazy dream, I was the one running away from everything, and Flynn had simply become that one point of focus to help me find my way back home. Strange indeed.

ON A RATHER MANIC Monday, word was circulating throughout the North Star offices about a pizza and drinks gathering taking place that Wednesday evening at Russo's Pizzeria, not far from our office.

In the past, whenever these social events were held, I generally took little notice and gladly opted out, sparing myself the torture of small talk. At least, that was how I perceived it. Barring the occasional after-work drink with a colleague or two, I did my best to avoid any group gatherings, formal or informal, always making an excuse to exclude myself, and instead headed back home where the comfort of solitude awaited me.

However, on this Monday, while I sat with my head buried in my laptop, I was suddenly greeted by Chiemi Amano, a fellow staff writer at Narrator, who appeared at my workstation. Chiemi was a woman my age, with jet black hair, very attractive, with a highly outgoing and warm personality. Despite my slight infatuation with Chiemi, she had been dating her current boyfriend for some time, but I'd heard they were currently on a break. I was always very attracted to Chiemi, yet because of circumstances and my determination to remain hidden away, my secret infatuation for her had remained just that, staring from afar and never revealing anything to anybody.

Hence my surprise when Chiemi appeared before me, asking me with some level of enthusiasm if I would be attending the Wednesday evening soirée. I couldn't help myself—I said I would be, and that I would look forward to seeing her there. Yet I felt doubtful that I would ever take it upon myself to say anything to Chiemi about my interest in her, as I was quite certain that she saw me only as that harmless guy friend in the office who keeps to himself and goes largely unnoticed.

When Wednesday evening rolled around, I went for a short walk through the streets of London, allowing my wandering mind to do its thing. Walking through the city was not the best environment to contemplate one's life, but that is exactly what happened—with my focus falling on my past relationship with Julia. It had been a long time since I had any type of romantic partner, as the breakup of my relationship with Julia had proven difficult, and I was worried that I might be doomed to make the same mistakes over again.

I made my way towards Russo's Pizzeria with a sense of anticipation. Evening had turned into night, and the lights of the city had brought a vibrancy to the busy streets, with people scampering about, and the sound of traffic and conversations of passersby resonating in harmony, creating a peculiar symphony.

As I approached Russo's from the opposite side of the street, I quickly glanced over before crossing and caught sight of Chiemi walking together hand-in-hand with her boyfriend, Ian Emery, whom I had met on a previous occasion. Once I crossed the road, I hesitated before entering, and instead edged my way to the right side of the large front window, keeping myself somewhat hidden, yet ensuring I could safely look inside without being spotted. I even went as far as to raise my phone to my ear under the pretense of holding a conversation, in case I was caught red-handed and forced to join in.

As I peered in, I could see quite a large group gathered at the far back of the restaurant. Chiemi and her boyfriend Ian had just sat next to Jenny Street, one of our lovely admin workers. I stood for a moment, being careful not to reveal myself, and looked in until such a point when I saw Chiemi and Ian share a kiss.

I stood with my back to the wall for a moment, as the sounds of the street symphony played in my ears, and I remained there almost frozen, lost in thought, unable to make a clear decision as to what to do. Why not just stroll in, say my hellos, eat some pizza, drink some beer, and have a good laugh with my colleagues? But I remained with my back to the wall, finally snapping out it for fear of being spotted by a colleague.

So, as I stared out at the busy street, I made the decision to walk away and go home, unsure exactly why I didn't go inside and join in. Maybe it didn't feel right, maybe I was just feeling antisocial, or maybe I didn't really have a place at that table.

FOLLOWING ON FROM THE pizza night, I was back in Olivia's office the next day, pondering a question she had posed to me regarding my decision to relocate back to England.

"I'm curious, what was it like to leave one's life behind and start over again?"

I smiled, thinking about my encounter with Brennan Brewer. After reflecting upon my own move, I suppose there were several reasons why I left and moved to England—not least the lure of a job, which had promised me professional growth and new opportunities to expand my writing portfolio.

It was a good and fair question Olivia had asked, and I felt it deserved a robust response. She was more than curious and, like many of her targeted questions, there was a place she wanted me to travel—even if it meant a somewhat rambling response to get there.

Following my father's death, I finished my education, started working in the Chicago area, and got stuck into my routine. There was really nothing else that was noteworthy in terms of my life over there, as I withdrew from family life, social life, and instead sought out the safety of my running and living in my small apartment. When I left the States, I had no friends, mainly a self-inflicted state of my own creation. For some time, I tried to live a life based on how I saw others living, and found myself adopting personae that I felt would make me more acceptable to those around me. That, combined with some general job dissatisfaction, led me away from my hometown and over to England for the purposes of reinvention and life-changing opportunities.

The move over to England was relatively straightforward, emptying my apartment of the few possessions I owned, plus disposing of a large accumulation of both private and professional paperwork, which led me to my backyard meeting with Jack Mattio—a running partner who owned a rather nice house not too far from me in the Chicago area. After sharing details of my vast volumes of unwanted paperwork, Jack invited me over to his house one Saturday to have a few beers and to set my papers alight in his backyard fire pit.

On that Saturday, Jack stoked the fire with kindling and small logs, and once the blaze took hold, I threw bags of paperwork upon the fire and sat back, watching it all burn, staring at the flames, drinking my beer, and wondering where my life in England would take me. When we were finished, there was nothing left but gray ash—every trace of my life in America was gone, and when I moved, I remembered that moment so well, burning everything down, every memory, every moment, every part of a life that once was. Afterward, when I met people in England, I never spoke of my past and it worked well, because most people didn't want to know anyway. I had a new life in England, and my past was pretty much irrelevant and left behind.

When I had finished my story, Olivia looked over at me and for once I was certain I recognized the sadness in her expression.

"Your paper-burning story did make sense. You saw it as an analogical episode, so yeah it makes sense that you held on to that memory. It's fascinating, but you know what—you don't need to burn down the world around you to find meaning and purpose in your life. Instead of burning it all down, try becoming a participant and not just an observer."

It was an interesting observation on Olivia's part, and as I left her office that day, I felt that much wiser, and a little more aware of my past motives as to why I had set alight the path behind me, erasing all details of a life once lived.

16

It was Saturday and I awoke to a very gray, rainy and dismal day in London, and with nothing too demanding on my agenda, other than some routine chores which could well be deferred to a later date, I decided it would be a good time to have a clear out of three box files that had found their place upon my writing desk. If I was going to become serious about my writing, it was time I tackled this project, did a bit of de-cluttering and reorganization, and returned the desk back to a usable state.

The desk, constructed of a simple solid oak top attached to a black metal frame, along with an office chair and a plain silver desk lamp, had been purchased for me by my mother at an office reclamation center when she came to visit shortly after my move back to England. Despite my initial objection, she was quick to point out that somebody who writes for a living should not be seated at a small and cramped kitchen table trying to construct meaningful manuscripts. After further debate, I felt forced to capitulate, eventually yielding to her generous offer.

After breakfast and a quick shower, I took the brave step to start my Saturday morning project, first tackling the blue box file by emptying the contents onto the desktop, sorting through an array of paperclips, pads, pens and pencils, rulers, rubber bands, pages from a long-abandoned novel I had started, and an odd assortment of miscellaneous items. I also found a few odd coins hidden away at the bottom of the file, plus some old bills and receipts that had somehow found their place amongst the chaos. I even discovered a small, mysterious key that to this day remains a mystery as to what it might open.

It soon became one of those tasks that I wished I hadn't started, but after reorganizing the first file and disposing of all that was not needed, I moved on to the red box file, again emptying the contents onto the table. As I began to sort through the mess that lay scattered in front of me, I smiled, thinking back at myself cramming every odd bit into these files without taking much notice of what was going on. I made a commitment as I worked my way through the mess to not allow this to happen again, once I had brought order to this chaos—but only time would tell.

Placing everything into the existing categories was proving useful, and I was moving through this file much quicker than I had with the first one. This file contained more paperwork than the first, including bank statements, old utility bills, an array of small notes and various scraps of paper, forcing me to read each one, upon which were written small reminders to myself, most of them work-related.

Mixed into the heap, I came upon a folded piece of paper. Once unfolded, I stared down at the small note with a complete sense of disbelief.

Written upon this small piece of paper, in beautiful penmanship, was a single word.

Snapdragon.

For a few moments I became lost in my thoughts, trying to make sense of what I had just discovered. There in front of me was the paper that I remembered so well, and the word that Sophie had elegantly written out and handed to me as we stood together in Garibaldi Square. I was quick to examine the flip side of the paper, remembering that she took the paper back and wrote her phone number on the reverse side. But to my disappointment, the reverse side was blank. How could this be? I clearly remembered her writing her number down on the reverse side of the note. It made no sense, yet the note was there with 'snapdragon' on it, just as I had remembered.

There was no explanation to any of it, other than Sophie was not a construct of my imagination as had once been suggested—she must exist. Somebody had clearly given me this note, and it must have been this mystery woman. I sat for over an hour, hoping that this discovery would trigger my memory, yet as before I was unable to recall any moment in my life when this note was given to me. How would this simple name of a flower on a small piece of stationery help me find her? I had begun to accept that Sophie was gone, would not be found, convincing myself that obsessing over her image was simply a waste of time, yet incredibly this small note—which had found its way into a messy box file—had brought it all back to me.

My mind was swimming with possibilities, even though I was no closer to finding her than I had ever been before. I didn't remember putting the note in this box file, but there it was. When did I place it there? Was it on the top of the heap when I emptied the box file onto the table? This was the top box file, so I must have put this note in there recently. Where had I been when I was given it? Why was there no phone number on the back?

I had to share my incredible find with somebody, to let others know about my discovery. It was too early to phone my mother, so I quickly phoned Flynn, who was at home with Emily and the baby. I apologized for my phone call, as I could hear Lizzy crying in the background, but once I told him of my discovery, he was as stunned as I was.

"Wow, dude. Get over here, I wanna see this note. You don't remember anything, nothing familiar about it?"

I assured Flynn I had no memory of any of it and didn't even remember how it ended up in that box file. In some ways this proved even more unsettling, as I thought that maybe that blow to the head had done more damage than I had realized, though I'd been given all assurances that this wasn't the case.

When I arrived at Flynn's home, the scene was one of family bliss, or chaos. Emily was scurrying around the house, holding the baby, with Flynn getting some food together at the same time as doing some dishes. I quickly shared the note with both Flynn and Emily, as neither of them could believe what I had discovered. Flynn studied the note closely, inspecting both front and back as I had, hoping to find some clue as to who wrote it hidden somewhere on the small piece of paper. I assured him that I had studied the paper closely, very closely, even feeling the texture of the paper, yet the truth remained elusive.

Flynn was excited about the discovery, as much as I was, but I told him that I was as far away from knowing who she was than ever before. I had a small piece of paper with one word written on it that I saw in a winding dream narrative, and that was it. Still, it had to be the mysterious woman of my dream who handed it to me…it just had to be. Yet, I had no idea who she was, or if she even existed.

I ran home in the rain from Flynn's house, still in a state of disbelief at my discovery. This peculiar breakthrough had brought it all back—her face, voice, mannerisms and even the touch of her hand in mine. It had come alive, and those details of my dream, though put aside, had not faded. She worked for her father's business, but what was it? She went to college in France, was proficient in languages, and wanted to start her own business. Yet, it was all still images and words in a dream, and just possibly a red herring leading to nowhere, as Olivia had previously suggested. It might have just been my mind creating a story to help me through that wandering and unsettling dream. But, despite the logic of it all, that image of Sophie and myself traversing the streets of Nice lived on. I had convinced myself that the answers were in Nice. Her name was Sophie, and we were together within some mixed-up dream state, and now she was gone.

I ran that night in a steady rain, trying to clear my head and find my balance once again. This strange discovery had unsettled me, leaving me with yet more questions and a complete sense of bewilderment. Despite being soaked through, I felt refreshed and awake. Once home, and after a long hot shower, I placed the one-word note on my end table, sat back on the sofa, and thought of it all again, convincing myself that it was time to move on. My search for Sophie was over, and despite the hopefulness of discovering the note, it was time to let it all go—or else this senseless quest would continue to torment me, despite my commitment to move on.

As Olivia had said, it was time to become a participant in my own life. I was tired and as I sat back, my body gave in to the exhaustion, and I could feel myself falling into sleep—but before I did, I remembered Sophie's face and heard her voice calling my name, and with that, I slept.

On the following Thursday, I met with Olivia for my usual appointment. I had been anticipating this session, wanting to tell her of my incredible discovery, and to see if together we might possibly uncover some lost clue as to where the note came from. I had exhausted all possibilities myself, thinking of every potential candidate who could have reason for writing the word 'snapdragon' down on a small piece of paper. There was nothing that rang familiar, and the process of trying to remember became frustrating for me, even to the point of complete exasperation.

Olivia sat looking over at me, smiling ever so slightly, waiting for me to finish the story of my discovery. I was anxious to get her take on the whole thing, as she had helped with all of this before—I was hoping at the least she would have some words of wisdom that might enlighten me.

She finally sat back in her chair in a very relaxed manner and looked at the note, giving me hope that she might provide some earth-shattering insight to help me solve this mystery once and for all. However, she followed up with only a rather simplistic inquiry.

"When you discovered the note, what was it that you felt, what you experienced in those moments after?"

An interesting query, and not what I thought Olivia would ask at this point.

"I don't know. I guess, excitement, dismay, disbelief, and above all, I felt hopeful—that maybe somewhere on this little piece of paper was an answer, or a clue, something that would trigger my memory. And then, I began to feel a bit unsettled, because even though this note was real, I realized in the end that it was merely a word on a scrap of paper and nothing more. It didn't lead me to anything new, and some of the hope and excitement began to fade. I think that blow to my head was worse than I thought. Why can't I remember?"

"I don't know if the accident contributed to this or not. But who knows, maybe that note was given to you shortly before your accident—memories close to an event such as you experienced might be lost. Do you think it's possible that when you were given this note, you closed your mind off to what might have been and simply dismissed it all? I'm not convinced that this whole lapse of memory is a result of the accident. I think there could be some other reason, like an emotional block."

I felt completely at a loss as to how to respond. Maybe she was right; could this truly be the reason I couldn't remember? It could have been a possibility, as maybe there was an interaction with somebody who, for whatever reason, handed me that note, and I simply couldn't be bothered to take any notice. But after pondering Olivia's question, I concluded that this was not the type of person I had become. I would never ignore or dismiss someone, and I would never minimize or trivialize anything that someone else had clearly identified as being important. None of it made sense, and I needed Olivia to understand.

"I don't know if I can make anybody see what I have been going through. It's like looking at a photo of myself and another person, and I can't remember who that person is, or where the photo was taken, or who took it, or anything else about it. I don't know what would happen if I did find this person. Who knows? I don't think I have any expectations—I just want to know. Maybe she didn't give it to me, maybe the woman down at the nursery or flower shop gave it to me, or maybe my neighbor Mrs. Dobbs gave it to me, it just doesn't matter—I just want to remember."

"Well, the discovery of the note certainly deepens the mystery. It's an incredible discovery and I don't want you to think that in any way I was trivializing what it means to you. It's just that you've worked hard in your sessions with me, and you've accomplished a lot. Just don't get sidetracked with it all. This mystery note that Sophie handed to you, well personally, I would buy a little frame and stick that note in there and put it somewhere to remind yourself of the beautiful mysteries that life holds for us all."

I couldn't help but ask, "Olivia, you believe Sophie is real and gave me that note? You just said it."

Olivia looked over at me with the most mischievous smile on her face, and simply raised her eyebrows. This simple response proved enlightening. It brought a smile to my face too, and a sense of hope that not all was lost. So, for now, I had accepted the fact that my search had ended—it was destiny's turn to make the next move.

17

The time came when the perspective about my life and the choices I had been making were beginning to shift, due in part to my work with Olivia, but also because of the time I had spent reinvesting in my own life. Change was happening, but like anyone, moments of uncertainty and self-doubt would often corner me, forcing me to retreat to that place of refuge where I sought safety and escape.

Understanding that desire and the need to move out of my comfort zone, I identified key areas of my life that needed my attention and commitment. They were rather basic objectives, but they helped me prioritize where best to put my energy, and I wrote them down and placed them on the wall near my desk so I would remind myself of these life responsibilities. Living a good and healthy life, including work/life balance, opening myself back up to others—especially to family, colleagues, and the few people I called friends—and looking forward, not focusing on my past mistakes. Finally, my last goal was to write my novel. Uncomplicated and straightforward, these were the objectives that would hopefully guide my life.

One evening after a long run, I opened the laptop and started writing the first paragraph of my novel, a creative endeavor that I had long desired to undertake, sharing the adventures of a long-distance runner by the name of Aaron Sleet. Aaron was to be my alter ego in part, a risk-taker endowed with courage and the strength to overcome adversity, while undertaking life-changing, transformative experiences. It would be a testament to Aaron's character, as he navigated the challenges of life with a sense of boldness and confidence. My enjoyment of creating characters and bringing them to life was always there inside of me, but all too often my refusal to carry on was born out of frustration and a lack of confidence, eventually abandoning my projects in lieu of sitting back and doing nothing. The process of creating a completed manuscript felt daunting and seemed like an insurmountable mountain to climb, and as a result closing the laptop and walking away became the easy way out. Yet when I would do this, I would think back to my very first creative writing class and the number one rule my professor shared with the students—never wait until you feel inspired to write, because it may never happen. But I felt a sense of renewal now—I wasn't writing for anybody else, just myself, and I was determined that I would value and enjoy the process of it all, no matter how tall the mountain.

As I sat back with my desk lamp illuminating the materials strewn around the desktop, and with thoughts and ideas swirling around in my head, and my first paragraph leading the way, my life as a storyteller had commenced. The road ahead would require research, hard work, sacrifice, and my full commitment, but I felt ready.

Flynn's peculiar sense of humor would often manifest in the most surprising ways, so when an unaddressed envelope dropped through my mail slot one Thursday evening, my instincts immediately alerted me to one of Mr. Warner's potential escapades. Once opened, a handwritten invitation to a Sizzling Fajita early dinner at the Warner household was inside, some gold paint adorning the edges of the makeshift invite. My curiosity got the best of me and so, after a quick phone call, I made my way over to their place to discuss the details.

Both Flynn and Emily were aware of my best efforts to keep social contacts at a minimum, so I was always on the lookout for any ruse or ambush that these two may have orchestrated, hoping to lure me into some type of trap or unwanted dating encounter.

"Don't worry about it dude," Flynn said to me, "it's only John, Marie, and Melissa. No big deal. They want to see the baby, so it's an early dinner and a few drinks afterward, nothing crazy. So quit worrying."

John and Marie were a married couple and long-time friends of the Warners, and Melissa, a pharmacist and exercise fanatic, went way back with Emily to their school days. Flynn and Emily had more friends than I could imagine, most of them interesting and colorful characters—many of them artists whom Flynn had met during his travels.

Emily was adamant Melissa and I would be the perfect couple, given our shared passion for running and love of sports. Melissa was indeed an avid runner, keeping a detailed log of weekly miles and along with her cycling and swimming, she was quite involved with endurance competitions.

Initially, I had declined the invitation, but Flynn was like a dog with a bone and wouldn't let this one go. Recently, however, I was feeling a desire to build a more fulfilling social life and decided this small affair would be a good opportunity to enjoy a chilled evening with some friends. I had been in Melissa's company several times before, and for the most part she was a lot of fun and a great conversationalist. She was tall with short cropped dark hair, and looked not unlike an Olympic athlete. Flynn insisted I would be a good training partner for Melissa and possibly more, yet I found her passion for running and exercise bordering on addictive, which didn't fit with my laid-back routine.

In the end, as much as I recognized that Melissa and I might be a good match in many respects, there was something about her that reminded me of Julia—for whatever reason I couldn't shake that feeling, and it scared me a bit.

Saturday rolled around quickly and once dressed in my white shirt, gray sweater, somewhat worn-out jeans and red running shoes, I made my way over to the Warner residence with an abundance of drinks and snacks for the group. Upon my arrival, Flynn informed me that the other guests were already there, with drink in hand.

As I entered the living room, Emily was standing holding the baby, with Melissa next to her staring down at Lizzy, while John and Marie looked comfortably well-placed on the two-seater sofa. As I greeted Melissa, my eyes were instantly drawn to her lovely figure, accentuated by her short black dress. Once we had settled in, my eyes were constantly drawn to Melissa, who looked stunning this evening—a side of her I had never quite seen in the past.

After our very enjoyable Mexican dinner, we retired to the living area once again, sharing laughs and lively conversation and some post-meal drinks—excluding Emily of course, who was off alcohol while breastfeeding. At some point the conversation shifted over to my accident, and without any warning, Flynn shared what I had experienced during my stay in the hospital. Although all of them had previous knowledge of my accident, they were curious to hear the first-hand account. Trying to convey the details of a rather erratic and unsettling dream that involved a wandering search for Flynn was not easy, yet John, Marie, and Melissa all seemed gripped by my story.

Flynn was also anxious to tell them about the mystery woman and the note I found in my desk, which led to numerous questions—each of the group clearly fancying themselves as amateur sleuths. They were curious about Sophie, each of them concluding that she must reside in Nice. As our little dinner party transitioned into an Agatha Christie-like scenario, Flynn suggested that we could create our own board game based on the story, with clues and all—it would make us millions.

It had turned out to be a nice evening and even though nobody was eager to leave, we all agreed it was best to end this party at a reasonable time—with Lizzy having just fallen asleep, it felt like the right time to make a move. Melissa was staying the night and Emily did her best to convince me to stay just a bit longer, but clearly I was still struggling to open those doors. The opportunity was there, but my mind wandered—something out there was calling to me, pulling me away from this room, while images of Sophie played on in my mind.

John and Marie's taxi had arrived, so I took the opportunity to say goodnight as well, much to Flynn and Emily's disappointment. As I walked home, I glanced upward and despite the local light pollution, the stars were bright and radiant. My gaze fixed upon this incredible display of cosmic wonder and mystery.

Once inside, I plopped down on the sofa, turned on the television and started watching the film *North by Northwest*. Though I liked the film, my mind was elsewhere—the discussion about Sophie, though lighthearted, had brought her back to life again. She was never far from my thoughts and while I knew moving on with life was the right thing to do, forgetting about my dream woman wasn't happening—at least, not for now.

18

Towards the end of November, my impulsiveness and newfound sense of wanderlust brought me back to my hometown, spending a week with my family just prior to Thanksgiving—flying out on a Monday and returning the following Tuesday. Unfortunately, work demands were such that I couldn't be there for Thanksgiving, my favorite American holiday, missing it by a couple of days, but my mother and sister were not to be deterred, and on Saturday evening, we would have our own celebration, including a big turkey and all the trimmings.

My week back in Chicago was everything I expected and more. I visited downtown with family, as well as taking some time on my own to run and walk around the familiar streets of Ravenswood. Whenever I visit the US, I find that emotions that have remained dormant for so long are suddenly reawakened and feed my longing to return there, finding my place once again amongst the familiar landscapes I left behind. It is often difficult to describe this experience to others—what's it like to miss the culture, the people, and the nuances of American traditions, even the vastness of the open sky. There is a special feel to one's homeland, an ambiance that connects you to a land and people that cannot be experienced while living in a foreign country.

Still, I knew that my life had come to a stop in Chicago, and when the opportunity arose to move to London, I was desperate to leave that life behind and hopefully begin the reinvention process—only to find myself repeating the same pattern, becoming emotionally detached and disconnected from the world around me.

Chicago, and the US in general, would always feel like home to me, and with my visit to the Upper Peninsula still very much alive in my mind, the desire to seek out life in small-town America continued to be very appealing. It was a difficult position being stuck between two countries, and I did find myself missing my family and life in America more and more, but moving back because my mom and sister were there would have been the wrong reason to do so.

Saturday proved to be as joyously busy as an actual Thanksgiving celebration, and after all the dust had settled, we all made our way to Robyn's living room where we played games, had some great laughs, and entertained Chloe and Richy as much as possible. At some point, Robyn had put on one of her classic playlists, insisting it was just background music, until such a time that she raised the volume, and we all took turns on the living dance floor to release our inhibitions and jump about. When Imelda May's song 'Tribal' came alive, Robyn and I teamed up, frolicking around the dance floor together hand-in-hand, being silly as we went, liberating ourselves. As we danced around the room, my mother, Peter, and the kids were ecstatic, laughing as Robyn and I tried to keep up with the pace of the music, celebrating this moment of abandonment before finally losing our collective balance and falling onto the sofa.

That night, as I lay in bed waiting for sleep to pay me a visit, I thought back over the past evening, and was grateful for all I had been given in life—despite some challenges along the way, I was fortunate to have had the support of two fantastic parents and a beautiful sister. There was so much to be thankful for, and I well understood a few rough patches along the way did not constitute a life of pain or suffering, not even close.

As I drifted off to sleep, I was grateful for the life, the loving family, and the opportunities I had been given.

THERE WAS A TIME, in retrospect, when my self-declared mission of finding Sophie had become a fixation that I could not shake, and despite my promise to move forward and get on with life, I had convinced myself that keeping the search going was the right thing to do. During my college days, coursework on investigative reporting offered me hope that my skills and background would provide me a springboard with which to uncover clues and identify avenues of exploration that might lead to the discovery of her identity.

Despite two trips to Nice for the purpose of conducting an in-person search of the area, and repeated searches on the internet, I had made the decision that it was best to let it go and get on with living. My work with Olivia had become quite significant in my choice to leave this all behind and despite reminders, including the note found in my cluttered red box file, I was moving away from it all, understanding the need to address priorities including career consideration and my work on a personal writing project. I had traveled some distance and, even though there was still work to do on my part, I was getting there and beginning to re-immerse myself in living.

However, through it all, there were those moments when my curiosity and the unresolved mystery would invite me back to continue the search, to seek answers to those questions that had left me wondering if my dream had resurrected somebody real, or if I was simply chasing a mental construct, an unreal image that had found its place amongst the pathways of my brain.

Just hours after I had returned from my family visit back to

America, I was suddenly drawn back into the mystery, when I discovered a text message from Antoine back in Nice.

Mike, something interesting I need to share with you. Can you please contact me? I attempted to phone you but had no success. Antoine from Nice

Upon reading the text, I was quickly overtaken with curiosity and excitement, yet I was careful to remain cautious and texted Antoine back, asking if I could phone or contact him via a video call. I felt impatient waiting for a reply, however within a couple of hours we were speaking face to face.

What followed was a fascinating set of events that Antoine described in as much detail as possible. In short, Antoine had a friend named Lucas, who had a friend named Samuel, and they all met recently on an evening out. It was Antoine's first-time meeting Samuel and at some point, during their night out, Samuel happened to say that he had a friend named Sophie who, along with her parents, owned a flower shop near Garibaldi Square. Still being alert to my desperate search, Antoine mentioned to Samuel that I was in search of a young woman named Sophie who had a real passion for flowers. Antoine was informed that Sophie had a house nearby, and that the family also had a regular place at the Cours Saleya market—the very one that I was familiar with. Antoine also told me that the young woman fit the description that I had shared with him.

As Antoine continued, I had to wonder if it was possible. Had I really met her so many years ago when I visited with Flynn and Emily, as we wandered through the market near the old town? More than likely, it was all just some odd coincidence—could a brief meeting about three years prior really leave such an embedded memory?

Antoine felt certain I could have met her as I wandered through the market, maybe having the briefest of conversations with her during a visit to her stall. We did stop at several stalls along the way, but I'm sure I would have remembered such a meaningful encounter. And what about the 'snapdragon' note—there had to be more to this meeting than a brief encounter. Unfortunately Samuel did not share any photos of his friend Sophie, however Antoine said it would be possible to get together with them this evening, and maybe we could all do a video call. Antoine was excited to help.

Thinking to myself that a simple photo of this woman from Antoine would suffice, I still found myself excited by the prospect of seeing this woman in person, so I kept silent and felt maybe this video call would be a good thing. Regardless of my own doubts and my reluctance to be dragged into yet more obsessive behavior, it all came home again, this sudden lighting strike—the possibility that this could be the woman who somehow managed to come and visit me while I lay sleeping in a London hospital room.

Again, it seemed unlikely that this was the woman of my dreams; it almost seemed too good to be true. Yet I was there in Nice with Flynn and Emily, and maybe Sophie and I had a chance encounter, however brief, that had made a lasting impression on me, leaving me with nothing but a fleeting memory, tucked away in the recesses of my mind, only coming to life as the result of a long and winding dream. The possibility existed.

"Antoine! Yes of course, I mean, who knows? I have so many questions for you, but there is no point until I see her. So, you haven't met her?"

"No, I haven't met her. Samuel thought it would be easier if we could talk to you, and if good fortune smiles upon you and it is indeed the woman that you met here, then you could ask the questions that you need to ask. I'm so glad I was able to get in touch with you. So, this evening at eight your time? They're coming to my place, so everything should work out."

"Yeah, fantastic. I'll contact you at eight. Take care for now."

It seemed so strange to not tell the entire truth to Antoine, but there was nothing to lose. If, by some mad twist of fate, it happened to be Sophie, then maybe all could be revealed, and I could finally get the answers I had been searching for. I went about the rest of that afternoon tidying up my apartment and doing some writing, waiting impatiently for time to pass—hoping I was about to speak with the woman who walked into my dream, introduced herself and asked kindly if I would watch over her flowers.

When the time finally arrived, a jumble of feelings had found their way to me, forcing me to compose and settle myself before our conversation commenced. If it was Sophie, would she recognize me, or would I simply be one of many faces who had crossed her path as she went about her business?

Antoine answered promptly and waved over his friend Samuel and the woman in question, my heart pounding as they took their seats next to Antoine.

"Mike, hello. This is my friend Samuel, and his friend Sophie."

Both Samuel and Sophie waived and said hello, and in those brief moments, I sat and stared at the woman on my screen, studying her lovely face ever so closely, as she kindly offered me a broad and generous smile. Her dark hair and beautiful eyes brought my dream back to life again, reminding me of that moment when a young French woman walked into my dream to say hello. However, the woman who sat with Antoine and Samuel was not the Sophie I had met in my dream, and as I smiled back and said hello, my heart sank—the anticipation and excitement that had abounded prior to my call, slowly began to dissipate.

After some conversation and a bit of question and answer about my dream girl, they each expressed their hope that I would find her one day. I said goodbye to Sophie and Samuel, thanking them for taking the time to talk with me, and told Antoine how much I appreciated his efforts in orchestrating this internet meeting.

Antoine hesitated before replying, "I'm sorry this didn't work out. I thought maybe we had hit the jackpot here, but it was not to be. Hey, one more thing, it would be nice if someday you could come over to Nice and I'll introduce you to my girlfriend and friends, and we can all spend some time together. There's some good nightlife over here, and my friends would like you, so please give it some thought."

"Thanks Antoine. I appreciate the offer, and I'll keep it in mind. So, let's keep in touch and well, I look forward to getting back over there someday. One last question before you go: how is Brigitte doing?"

Antoine laughed and seemed surprised that I remembered his beloved cat.

"She's fine, thanks for asking. She is pretty much an indoor cat now and only ventures out with me in her company, so yes, we're doing fine."

After we said our goodbyes and I sat back on my sofa thinking of what had just transpired, the sense of disappointment I had initially felt was replaced by an acceptance of the situation, and the outcome it delivered. This internet meeting did not unfold as I had hoped, yet I felt a sense of resolve and satisfaction that I was able to move through this moment without the weight of disappointment dragging me downward, and for that I was thankful.

STARING OUT OF OLIVIA'S office window at the falling rain felt therapeutic, with the sound of the raindrops offering a soothing respite after a frantic rush to my scheduled appointment, dodging traffic and navigating the busy streets of London to arrive on time. It was dark and moody outside, and the calmness and soothing lighting of Olivia's office was welcoming, providing me the opportunity to simply sit and relax.

Olivia was quick to pick up on my appreciation for rainy days, asking, "What is it you like about this weather?"

"Um…the sound, the calmness of it all. It stills the chaos of a busy world a bit and slows everything down. I like running in the rain, as long as it's not a downpour. I even downloaded extended rain audio clips that I listen to, and my sister bought me a rain CD years ago. So yeah, I like it, very calming."

"Speaking of your sister, how was your visit back to Chicago?"

"It was great. I spent time with my mother and sister and her family, and really enjoyed it all. I miss my mother a lot and it made leaving difficult. We had a Thanksgiving dinner together on the Saturday before I left—turkey and all the trimmings—and it was like old times again. That evening, we played games and my sister put one of her playlists on, and we all just danced around the living room floor, just being silly. At one point, Robyn and I danced together, and we just let go. We were so close when we were younger, but our relationship matured, and I suppose like most people, those kinds of silly moments got lost along the way. But, yeah, it was nice."

"Why was that evening especially meaningful to you?"

It took me a moment to recollect in detail what I was feeling at the time.

"I guess it was the warmth and fun of it all, and I felt connected to my family again. I hadn't felt that in a long time."

Being with Mom and Robyn and the family, and being back in Chicago, I had forgotten what it was like, and I didn't want to leave. After my father died, I avoided those times—family celebrations and such felt wrong, like I had no right to be there without him.

Sometimes I thought maybe my mom and Robyn blamed me for not being with my father when he went to that conference, and I had a hard time facing them. I shared that with them a while back, and they were saddened that I would have ever thought that. But in the process of it all, I drifted away from the two of them.

Olivia took a moment before she spoke.

"Blaming yourself for what happened to your father and separating from them was just part of the life pattern you were living. Spending time with your mom and dancing with your sister and missing them all just proves that despite the tragedy that beset you all, those valuable moments are still out there."

After some time, Olivia was curious as to my progress with the early stages of my novel. She wanted to better understand what it was all about.

"My novel, well, it's about this guy who runs and is out there, sometimes on the edge of the world doing his thing, meeting some interesting people and discovering liberation in the process."

"Wow, sounds familiar. What does your main character look like? I mean, what's he like?"

"Well, he's a compilation of sorts, including a bit of myself—the running part I suppose. I still have a ways to go on his development."

"What's his mission going to be like? What are these adventures going to look like?"

"I don't know yet. I mean, I could make this guy whatever I want—heroic, risk-taker, adventurer—he could be anything. He'll have some flaws, but one thing for sure he will encounter some rickety bridges along the way, only he will more than likely cross them without any hesitation, unlike my own struggles to get over. I want my character to have the strength to manage adversity, and the courage to do what he has to do to cross those bridges."

It was at that point that Olivia said something to me that was both simplistic, yet incredibly meaningful.

"You know, in everybody's life—we all get stuck along that rickety bridge at some point. Don't be fooled by those who say they don't because it's just not true. It's just knowing how to manage the swinging and rickety bridge in the end, and how best to go forward or go back the way you came. Either way, moving forward or choosing to retreat, we're all very capable of making the right choices for ourselves. We can create heroes or alter-egos who bravely face those challenges, but in reality, life isn't always that black and white."

When I walked from Olivia's office that day, I felt a sense of commitment I hadn't experienced for a long time. I would choose the direction I wanted to move in and only when I was ready and willing—not according to anybody else's expectations. I was still finding my way back, but as I stood aloft on that fragile, rickety bridge I had walked along, I was more confident, ready to move across. Whatever awaited me on the other side, and whatever the outcomes of my choices, I felt prepared to take the risk.

Flynn's artistic project began to gather some momentum, and on Saturday afternoon he had planned another gathering at his house including three of his friends from Paris who were visiting and staying in London for a long weekend. Flynn thought it would be a good opportunity for me to gather information and talk with his friends about the project. My work on the article had been delayed due to other work commitments, but the intent was to move forward with it as soon as possible, which would more than likely include a couple of trips over to Paris.

Flynn had also invited John, Marie, and Melissa once again and he described this event as being an afternoon of fun, with a little shop-talk thrown in amongst the mix. Flynn loved entertaining others, and despite now having a baby, he was not to be deterred from socializing with friends. Both Emily and Flynn had insisted I attend. However, on Friday and after some serious contemplation, I phoned and told them that I had some serious work deadlines and Saturday just wasn't going to work for me. As expected, I was met with some formidable opposition, but despite my commitment to open myself up to more social engagements, sitting with others and engaging in small talk was not at the top of my agenda. Telling Flynn a looming work deadline was keeping me at home was the best excuse I could muster, even if I was more likely to be sitting on my sofa watching YouTube videos.

As it turned out, Saturday proved to be a productive day—I became immersed in my ongoing novel, losing myself in thought as I tried to imagine what new challenges may be awaiting my adventuresome protagonist, Aaron Sleet. As day turned into evening and darkness descended, I felt a run was in order after sitting at my laptop most of the day.

As I ran on, I experienced a sense of euphoria as I had on previous running excursions. Many tried to dispel the runner's high as a myth, but I knew it to be real and on more than one occasion I had experienced a sense of delight and outright joy because of it. It was with me that evening as I ran on, pushing me forward, liberating me, if only for the length of my run.

I thought of what Olivia had said to me on Thursday: "We all get stuck along the rickety bridge at some point. Don't be fooled by those who say they don't because it's just not true." This statement left a strong impression on me, and reminded me that as individuals, we are all human and subject to those moments of vulnerability and uncertainty, unsure as to how best move forward or backward.

For so long I had pounded away at myself, needlessly and almost mercilessly, unforgiving of my past decisions, transgressions, and mistakes, becoming stuck along the way, unable at times to move forward or backward and feeling undeserving of anything good or fortunate that might come my way. I often fooled myself by keeping occupied, distracting myself through overwork, watching endless sports on television, and filling every bit of free time with senseless chores and nights out with work colleagues, convincing myself that I was living a life with purpose. Olivia once said, "Just because you keep moving, doesn't necessarily mean you're getting anywhere."

My life, summarized perfectly in one sentence—going through the motions of living, but still stuck in the same endless loop. It was what my life had become.

Once back home, I had a bit of late dinner, settled back in my comfortable sofa, and watched some travel videos on YouTube, hoping to gather further inspiration for my heroic adventurer as he made his way running around the globe. When my evening finally ended and before I made my way off to bed, I glanced over at the small, framed note on my end table, and thought again of Sophie's lovely face, and felt grateful for the message she had left behind.

My day had ended and as I lay in bed that night, I once again felt thankful—for the life I had been given—for my family, the few good friends I had, and for finally having the courage and faith to start crossing that rickety bridge.

19

It was the very end of November when I woke to a chilly but very sunny Saturday morning. I had accepted an invite to meet a fellow writer by the name of Willis Henry for a late morning coffee. Willis, who lived close to London, was a freelance writer whom I had met about a year ago when we crossed paths at a writers' event in the city. Willis was in his late thirties and married with two young children, and was in the challenging position of balancing a career in writing along with family responsibilities.

Willis and I had met up a couple of times in the past to chat about the writing business, and comparing notes was always useful to me, as my interest in going freelance was beginning to feel like a more concrete possibility. He was also a huge fan of British history and had been doing a significant amount of research in preparation for writing a historical novel that he had mapped out some time ago.

I headed towards Covent Garden where we were to meet at one of the many coffee shops in the area. However, once on my way, I received a phone call from Willis apologizing profusely, stating that he had a bit of an emergency on the home front and had been lumbered with childcare duties as his wife had a hair appointment, which he had completely forgotten about.

After assuring Willis it was not an issue, saying we could always meet up some other time, I decided to head down the Strand over to Drury Lane. I liked that area of London, with all its shops, pubs, restaurants, and theaters squeezed together into such a small space. Drury Lane had become a stopping point of mine on occasion, as several of us from work would often make this our rendezvous point for a quick breakfast or lunch. As much as I had wanted to meet up with Willis, in the end I was glad for the opportunity to take a leisurely walk around London and not worry about being somewhere at a certain time.

The area around Drury Lane was buzzing with all sorts wandering around, filling the small cafés, eateries, and coffee shops along the way. There were even some braving the cold temperatures sitting outside having a smoke and a chat, while others appeared comfortably tucked away inside, escaping the November chill. After dodging and weaving my way over to Queen Street, I walked along the road trying to find the least busy place where I could sit and relax for a while. Eventually I came up to the Open House Café, which appeared busy with several people sitting outside under the large colorful awning, but upon glancing inside I could see a few empty tables, and after my dash to the counter and ordering my morning coffee and almond croissant I found a seat on the far side of the café, up against the wall. I had been in the Open House several times before, stopping in for a quick hot drink and pastry, mainly because I liked the chilled ambiance, the smells of coffee and pastries as you walk through the door and the quaint décor that brought so much character to the place. Despite my promise to become a more active participant in life, I still valued the opportunities to sit and observe, my anonymity safeguarded, as those around me went about their lives in the mainstream. As habits go, I laid my phone on the table and fell into the trap of looking at pretty much nothing, as I scrolled through old messages, photos, news, and whatever else might catch my attention. A digital detox was long overdue, recognizing that I often ignored the warning signs of becoming complacent and even dependent upon my smartphone, and the various social media sites that offered me distraction and escapism.

As life went on around me, I found myself looking at a short video clip of Flynn changing a diaper amidst a floor covered in paintbrushes, paints, and whatever else he had lying around in his studio. It brought a smile to my face as I watched the incredible life transformation that Flynn was undertaking, managing it all so well as he looked up and laughed at a giggling Emily, who was behind the camera.

Oblivious to what was happening around me, and with my head down, smiling at Flynn's gallant effort to change his daughter's diaper, what happened next can barely be conveyed through the written word. As I continued to appreciate Flynn's determination, the silence in my little corner of the world, in this little corner of London, in this little corner of a busy café, was suddenly broken by a songbird—a calming and reassuring voice from somewhere in my past that drifted through my head and left me frozen.

The feminine voice, the cheery tone, and the unmistakable and alluring French accent could have belonged to only one person.

"Excuse me," this songbird proclaimed, "but I think you're the young man that stood me up so very long ago."

As I looked up, I sat and stared in complete disbelief—for in front of me stood Sophie, the girl of my dreams, the elusive character of my narrative, who guided me and offered me comfort during my mystical, confusing search.

I was dumbfounded and unable to immediately respond, struggling to comprehend how this beguiling woman could be standing in front of me, smiling down at me, coffee in hand and looking as beautiful as I remembered her. There was no detail of her I had forgotten—her beautiful face, her jet-black hair woven into a braid, and that most alluring and disarming smile. She was dressed as I would expect, wearing a heavy, colorful cardigan, a yellow scarf, jeans, and blue running shoes.

Upon standing, my legs almost failed to keep me upright.

"Oh my God, Sophie?"

It was all I could muster as I forced myself to remain steadfast despite being unable to make sense of what was happening in front of me.

Sophie's expression shifted to one of concern and confusion, as it became apparent that she was struggling to understand or comprehend my reaction.

"Are you okay? I hope I haven't upset you. I wasn't even sure if you would remember me—I mean, I still have your name written down in my diary. I left it there, so when I see it, I often wonder what happened to you."

I ran my hand over my face, trying to reassure myself that I was not dreaming again, that this moment was real, that it was all happening in the here and now. I felt puzzled by what she had just said to me, and I feared I would suddenly find myself jumping up in bed, tortured again by another reminder of somebody I once knew and could no longer find. But there she stood, in front of me, speaking to me, and that sudden jolt of disbelief and subsequent moment of anxiety had now come to pass.

"I'm sorry Sophie, I've been looking for you for so long. I need to explain something to you, it's something…" I became lost for words, but Sophie stood patiently, waiting for me to finish. "Can you sit with me? Do you have time to sit with me?"

The look on her face reminded me of the Sophie in my dreams, and without hesitation, she placed her coffee on the table and sat down.

"Yes, I have time."

Only then did we begin to talk. I was impatient to make her understand, to explain the journey, the confusion of a mixed-up dream, so before I had the chance to ask her how we met, I explained the accident, the injuries, and medical intervention, including the loss of a very key memory. Before I proceeded any further, I finally stopped and asked Sophie for the details of how we met.

Sophie smiled over at me before she replied, "You know, at first, I thought that's either one incredible story, or you were just desperate to come up with a quick excuse for standing me up—but I could see the distress in your face. I'm sorry about what happened to you."

Sophie, in detail, proceeded to tell me of the day we met. It was the Friday just before the Saturday when my family arrived in England. Sophie had walked along Drury Lane on her way to work, carrying a tray of snapdragons from a small flower market along the way, deciding to stop at the Open House Café for a cup of tea and a morning muffin, as she often did. Since it was busy inside, she happened to see a young man sitting on his own and thought maybe he could watch her flowers while she made her purchase at the counter.

Upon returning to the table, she sat with me and we talked for quite some time before she made the decision to finally leave for work. We said our goodbyes, but before she made her way out, she said I kindly offered to carry her tray of flowers for her.

"In fact," she stated, "you were very much the gentleman."

After further questioning on my part, Sophie told me in part how she ended up living in London. Upon completing her university education in France, Sophie landed in London working for the International School of Language Studies, a professional learning institution started by a consortium of partners including her own father, a French business owner. The school, located near Drury Lane, provided language courses to all, including business clients, many of whom were involved in global travel. Sophie explained that after university she worked for her father in Bordeaux, eventually accepting a role as a manager and teacher at the language school in London. She told me her family were language fanatics, with herself and her younger sister both being polyglots.

My question-and-answer routine was suddenly cut short when Sophie stopped me mid-question, saying, "You know, when we met on that day, and after you left, I knew little about you. I tried to ask you, but you were the one asking all the questions, and all I got from you was that you wrote for a living."

As Sophie continued, it all made sense to me—asking all the questions, while maintaining the right amount of distance to keep myself safe.

Sophie obliged my curiosity by continuing with the story of how we met. She said that when we reached her school on that day, I had told her I was planning a trip to France with a friend to cover a work assignment and that I wanted to surprise him by learning some French. Sophie had to go to Bordeaux for a few days to visit family, for her father's birthday, but said she was due to return the following Friday. We had agreed that I would come on that Friday afternoon, as there was an open house at her center, and we could talk about my interest in learning some French and then go out for a drink afterward. Sophie gave me a language school leaflet from her handbag with her number written on it, and the meeting time, and I promised her that I would be there, and was looking forward to seeing her. She then explained that her phone rang, and she got involved in a brief work conversation, and asked me to wait until she was done with the call. However, I gave her a wave and told her that I would see her on that next Friday.

After I'd departed, Sophie looked over and saw that leaflet she had given me lying on the edge of a nearby brick wall. She ran down the street, leaflet in hand, trying to find me, but I was gone, lost somewhere in the crowd. Sophie had no phone number for me, didn't know my last name, or even where I worked. When I didn't show up on that Friday, she thought I was simply not interested or perhaps had forgotten about our date.

After filling in the blanks, she had one last important detail to add.

"That note you have, the Snapdragon note, I gave that to you before we left the café. I quickly jotted it down on a small piece of paper, because you seemed interested in flowers. Anyway, when I saw you today, I had to say hello—of course I hadn't forgotten you, and I'm so sorry about your accident."

All I could do was nod at what she had told me, but none of it made sense to me.

"I think I'm the one that should be sorry. I'm just surprised you remembered me, especially somebody who you thought had stood you up. Why didn't I give you my phone number?"

Sophie's face lit up with a smile, and she replied, "Well, we didn't have much time to talk about work and all. It was all about flowers and such. You said you worked in London and wrote for a living, but I didn't know what you did, and you just kept asking me questions. You did tell me one thing—that your sister was a fantastic gardener and she really liked flowers as well. That's why I wrote down the name of them for you."

"Wow, I can't believe I didn't tell you what I did, or anything about myself."

"I did my best, but you were more interested in knowing about me—and my snapdragons of course."

"If you did think I had stood you up on that Friday, why did you come over to me today?"

Sophie thought for a moment before answering, "I don't know. I saw you there again, alone like last time, and when I met you on that day, there was something genuine and honest about you, and some sadness about you maybe. And even though you didn't come that day, well, I don't know. When I saw you today, I could have walked away, but I thought why not, why not see if that's the person I remember."

"I thought it was all lost, just this endless search…"

Sophie's expressions varied from complete surprise to disbelief and compassion, as I told and retold the story of my accident and my subsequent search for her. It was such a strange experience sitting with this beautiful woman, staring into her large brown eyes, oddly remembering it all from my dream—her smile, voice, and vibrant personality. I told her everything that had happened in my life since the accident, including the dream, my counseling experience, everything that would help her make sense of my situation. I focused on my search for her, my relentless internet search, any hopes of finding her amongst the many Sophie entries I had entered on my computer. There was still one question, however, that I needed to ask.

"I know we had met briefly, but how was it that you remembered me?"

"Oh, come on. I wouldn't forget. You were so lovely to me. You asked me if I would teach you some French, and you asked me out for a drink. You said your family was to be with you that week, but they would understand if you were out on that Friday evening. But your accident happened, making you a man of mystery. I had nothing, just a first name and no phone number."

Sophie seemed anxious to help me understand the circumstances of our initial meeting, to remind me of that very moment when our lives intersected at a small London café, as I sat alone, hiding away from the world around me.

"When you didn't show, I just thought you weren't interested.

And by the way, that day at the Open House, well I lied to you. I didn't randomly pick you out and ask you to look after my flowers. I saw you there and thought, well, he looks nice. I'm not one to just approach random strangers, so I took a bit of a risk with you. And when we talked, you were very sweet. Anyway, so, there you go."

"By the way, my first name is actually Lillian. It was my mother's grandmother's name, but my father never liked it—although he denies it to this day—so he always called me by my middle name, Sophie, and it stuck. It was what I answered to, so searching for Sophie on the internet, well, maybe that's why it all proved so difficult."

Sophie continued to tell me that on the day we met, we laughed as she regaled me with tales of gardening, snapdragons, and everything else. We then made our way down Drury Lane until we came to a small side street, and then to another small side street until we arrived at her place of work, where we made a date to meet up that next Friday at three in the afternoon, and then her phone rang. Why I never left a number wasn't really a mystery—it was just me standing in shadows, hiding in plain sight. Yet why was it I couldn't remember our meeting, only coming to life in a confusing and darkened dream?

Looking over at Sophie, I didn't want this day to end.

"Sophie, do you have to go? I mean, I could walk with you, or you know, or are you meeting somebody, or something?"

"I'm not meeting anybody, and I would appreciate talking to you a little more. I think I want to understand all of this, what happened to you and everything. I was just going into work today for a bit of a catch-up, but it can wait until Monday. We can just walk and talk, I mean it's beautiful out—cold but lovely. What do you think? Because I would like to hear more about this crazy dream of yours."

I smiled at Sophie and said, "Well, yeah, I'd like that. I just didn't know if maybe somebody was waiting for you."

Sophie laughed—a laugh I remember so well from within a very deep sleep.

"There's nobody waiting for me, and I don't have anywhere to be. I just want to hear your story, because it appears as though I had quite a role in it all. So, let's walk. Can we start here again? Hello Mike, I'm Sophie Allemand—so nice to meet you."

After our re-introductions, Sophie and I walked and walked until we decided it was time to get some lunch, and as we talked on, missing pieces of the puzzle began to reveal themselves to me, snippets of memory intermingled with my wandering dream. I remembered those moments, talking to her and feeling as drawn to her as I did now.

We shared stories from our past, and Sophie spoke of the break-up of her relationship with a man she had been with for two years.

"He was a barrister in Bordeaux, and I tried hard to make it work, but he wasn't interested, and he eventually found somebody he liked more than me, so he left."

When you live long enough, sadness will come one day to pay a visit. Sophie was no different than any of us—it was there within her, swirling about and mixing with all those other emotions that make us who we are, and can often dictate how we choose to live our lives. It can be difficult to offer consolation to someone we just met or barely know without it sounding empty or meaningless, but I wouldn't let that moment pass no matter who was sitting across from me.

"I know I just met you or met you for the second time, but I'm so sorry that happened to you."

"Thank you. But hey, life's not perfect, and not without its sad moments sometimes."

My curiosity was getting the better of me, but I didn't want

Sophie thinking I had made any assumptions about her current romantic status.

"I hope I'm not out of order by asking this, and I don't want to assume anything, but are you with anyone right now?"

"It's okay to ask. It took me a while to come back from the place I was in. I don't know, I just haven't made myself available. A friend sounds really good to me right about now. And since you asked, how about you?"

"No, no, it's been a long time. Yeah, I had a relationship that ended some time ago as well, and I guess I haven't made myself available either."

We talked on like old friends, before continuing with my familiar question-and-answer routine.

"So, tell me, your job here in London. I assume you like it here?"

"Well, I like it, but much of the reason for moving here was because I needed something different at the time. My father offered me this opportunity and I took it, and no regrets. I like London, and I like language and teaching others, and I get to manage part of it, so yeah, it's been good. But saying that, I don't know how long I'll do it. I think I would like to buy a small place in the French countryside, maybe, and just live a simpler life. It makes more sense to me."

Sophie's answer surprised me and, having nurtured my own small-town dreams, I wanted to know a little more.

"So, you don't like big city life?"

"My family moved to Paris when I was young and it was okay, and then when I got a bit older, we moved back to Bordeaux, where my parents are from, and we lived in the countryside. I like London, but I don't think I want to continue my life in a big city for very much longer. I'm kind of a homebody, if that makes sense. I like to work in my garden, cook, enjoy nature, walk, and just sit outside in the sun and read. But I guess it all depends on so many things.

Okay, I'm talking too much and you're asking all the questions once again—what are you thinking over there?"

"Well, being with you today, it's all so surreal. I'm not sure I can make you understand. You are from Bordeaux, not Nice, and all this time I invested in a mad search for you in Southern France. Okay, I'm going to tell you the truth and it's going to sound bizarre, but I even went to Nice, twice, thinking maybe I would see you there, that place where we met when I dreamed of it all. Yet, you were right here all the time. I can't make you understand what this dream was like, I couldn't make anybody understand it. When we met today at the Open House, for a moment, I was afraid I was going to wake up again, and it all would have been just another dream. And then today, you walked in, and my manic and frustrating search suddenly and unexpectedly came to an end."

When lunch ended, we wandered a bit more before finally calling it a day. We stood together in Covent Garden.

"Hey, I was wondering, would you be interested in having dinner or a walk in the park soon? I mean as friends. We could talk snapdragons and all. Maybe even a French language lesson."

Sophie laughed out loud and replied, "Yes, I would be very interested in having dinner or walking in the park, or both. I want to understand more about that wild journey of yours."

After we exchanged our phone numbers and agreed to a Wednesday evening date, I realized I had finally awakened from my dream. There was no retreating now, no going back and hiding in the shadows. I had become a participant in life again. This lovely and generous woman had walked into my life for a second time, and this time I would not let the opportunity slip away. Our time together ended, and a kiss on each other's cheek sealed the deal.

Before we went our separate ways, Sophie looked over at me with a mischievous smile, one that I remember well from a dream so very long ago.

"I have something important to tell you, so you better pay attention. If you slip and fall on the way home and bang your head and you forget about me and dream about me again, well, I'm in your phone now—so no excuses this time."

Before my beautiful mystery woman went on her way, there was this remembrance of a time past that needed to be shared.

"One last thing, mademoiselle—your perfume, it's lovely."

"It's essence of orange blossom. Glad you like it."

As I walked away, a smile came to my face. Finally, after such a long time, my elusive dream girl had found me once again, and the mystery was solved, discovering the answers that had evaded me for so very long. Sophie was real and she had been out there all along, somewhere in the hectic backdrop of London life. Thankfully she had the courage to reach out once more to that solitary figure, who sat alone, trying to steady himself upon a lengthy and very rickety bridge.

WHILE SITTING ON THE train back to Greenwich, I ran over and over in my mind the incredible event I had just experienced. I wanted to phone Sophie and hear her voice again, to remind me again that this mystery girl, who had eluded my best efforts to locate her, had indeed just walked back into my life—for a second time.

Yet as I sat and pondered it all, I began to wonder what had really happened after that very first time we met. Questions began to pull at me as I stared out the train window. Did I leave that leaflet on that brick wall on purpose? Did I simply walk away, afraid to step out of the shadows and bring myself into the world of the participants? Why was that memory lost to me after my accident? What was the reason for not writing down the date of our meeting in my work diary, or on my phone?

Was I afraid to go and see such a lovely young woman because of my own self-doubts and my inability, or unwillingness, to find my way out of the maze that I had so amply constructed? Was I continuing to punish and deprive myself of the possibility of discovering some semblance of happiness?

As the train rambled on and rocked its way down the tracks, I couldn't answer these questions. Why hadn't I told my mother or sister about my encounter with Sophie? I had the perfect opportunity to do so. Flynn and Emily knew nothing of her, so for that very short period between meeting Sophie and my unfortunate accident, I kept her a secret. Why did I do this? It makes sense that just maybe, I had no intention of going on that Friday afternoon to see this lovely woman who had walked into my life and offered me a sincere and genuine invitation to meet up and just be together for whatever reason. I couldn't make sense of any of it. I sat back and tried to understand my motives for not telling anybody or recording my date with her anywhere. And perhaps the biggest unanswered question of all remained—why did I place Sophie's snapdragon note amongst all that clutter in that box file? For what reason did I keep it? Here I was again, struggling to make sense of something that I had very little recollection of.

Despite replaying the hospital dream in my head, I still could not manage to see through the fog and understand what may have happened to me following my meeting with her on that very eventful day. I began to feel angry with myself, and the frustration of not being able to fully remember our initial encounter cast a sense of confusion as to what my actual motives may have been at the time. I must have kept her note for a reason and, possibly because of a hasty effort to tidy up before my mom and Robyn came, I simply shoved the note into the box file. There had to be something to it as

I just couldn't believe I would have walked away that easily. None of it made sense.

Yet despite all the questions without answers, the self-doubt, the possible motives at the time, and considering this huge mountain of uncertainty, somehow, we had met again. Sophie had walked my way once more, and good fortune had seemingly smiled down upon me for a second time. In between our two chance meetings, there had been an unfortunate event that stole the memory of our first meeting from me, and as a result, I remained a somewhat tortured soul, trying to unravel a mystery that left me with scattered images and no clues as to Sophie's identity, other than her name, a beautiful face, and a lovely French accent. For months, I had chased my own tail, trying to decipher what little information I had, while relying on a supportive therapist who encouraged me to push on with my own journey despite all the unanswered questions.

If I were to guess as to what happened after my first encounter with Sophie, I would say I had been afraid to go out in life, to experience living again, and possibly discover the prospect of finding peace of mind within the mainstream of life. For so long, I avoided people, women, intimacy, even my own family, being present in some respects, but simply going through the motions with a vacant mindset, almost void of emotion, keeping myself safe by living in a non-eventful world. I didn't care and didn't think I deserved anything good, and so my life had become a self-fulfilling prophecy, walking around standing on the outside – always looking in at a world I just didn't know how to enter. I was the observer, staring in at all the participants as they went about their lives, taking risks, trusting others, laughing, having fun, hugging loved ones, and embracing all those beautiful and cherished moments that life has to offer.

Later that evening I went out for a run, occupying my mind

with images of Sophie and reliving our conservation from today, and celebrating the fact that my search had finally come to an end. After months of seeking out any possible clue as to the identity of my mystery woman, all the while transitioning through personal change, in walked Sophie and my life changed in a moment. About five months had passed since our first encounter, and who could have guessed we would meet again in these circumstances?

Sophie and I had met again, thanks to her keen observational skills and persistence in finding an answer as to my disappearance. As we strolled through the streets of London, I recognized in Sophie a strong sense of determination, a tenacity that fueled her sense of optimism, allowing her to live a life full of confidence and purpose. Despite facing her own challenges in life, Sophie remained a participant, never yielding or surrendering in the face of adversity. In contrast, I had become stuck, a victim of my own self-talk and destructive thinking. I had indeed exiled myself, hiding away, denying myself in the process of any opportunity to find my way back to the mainstream of life.

Yet, ironically because of my search for this mystery woman, I began to find that purpose again—that confidence to go forth and seek out my place in this life, that very place that I had abandoned so long ago on a tragic and fateful day. It was all returning to me: the excitement, the willingness, and the determination to become that participant once again. The search for this elusive and beautiful woman had guided me back to a place filled with purpose and meaning. I had, indeed, returned.

I was anxious and excited for Wednesday to come, because finally, after a five-month search, the mystery of my dream narrative and the search for this beautiful woman had come to an end. It was time to celebrate the fact that this incredible mystery had finally faded away.

MY WEDNESDAY EVENING DINNER date with Sophie was everything I could have hoped for and more, as we sat and talked like old friends, sharing stories about life, work, and aspirations, and laughing ourselves silly for no apparent reason. We ventured into new territory, revealing aspects of ourselves generally reserved for longer-term relationships built upon a deeper sense of trust and understanding.

In my past, I often relied upon a cautionary strategy so as not to reveal too much information, for fear of compromising myself. However, due in part to the recent events of my life, I regained a welcome sense of clarity and began to understand that there does exist a line where courage, disclosure, and trust must play its part in creating a balanced approach to the early stages of healthy relationships, and those other basic connections with others. Because of this, and after sharing family photos during our dinner, I told Sophie the story of my father's tragic death, leaving nothing unsaid, explaining the details and circumstances of his morning walk, which led him to that fateful moment.

However, I didn't want our time together that evening to be overshadowed by sad or tragic stories, so we agreed that other such conversations would be deferred to another time, as this evening was a time to celebrate our wondrous reunion and revel in the incredible mystery of our two very serendipitous café encounters. After an extended dinner, we took a late evening walk around the streets of London, before catching our respective trains home.

My time with Sophie had been brilliant, and as I traveled home, I felt like I had discovered a friend and kindred spirit, two like-minded souls traveling through life who came together in the most fortuitous of circumstances, in the most unexpected of places. I offered silent thanks for those moments of synchronicity when Sophie walked into my world in that London café, and reached out to me as I sat alone, observing life from afar.

My time with Olivia was winding down and we had previously spoken about bringing my counseling experience to an end. However, we weren't quite there yet. There had been discussion about the distance I had traveled within the therapeutic process, and she was certain the time was nearing for me to move on. Throughout the process, Olivia had given me the opportunity to explore those difficult moments and to raise awareness around my self-isolation and the guilt, and unresolved grief, that had kept me stuck for so long. My entrenched behaviors and unwillingness to act had prevented me from moving out of a comfort zone of my own creation, which had kept me disconnected from the world around me. Early in the process, Olivia had told me that the awareness was there within me, but it required a commitment to face up to those challenges and move forward. That, more than anything, had defined my situation, and so I remained static, feeling it was safer to live in that comfort zone than it was to seek solutions and rejoin the real world.

I was under no illusion that these life struggles had come to an end, and despite Olivia's vote of confidence in me, we both knew that the negative self-talk might rear its ugly head from time to time, striking me during my most vulnerable moments. But I was prepared now and anxious to move on, leaving all those destructive thoughts behind me, and looking forward to a life full of aspiration and purpose. Thankfully I had the support of a very talented and caring therapist who provided me with the tools I would need to approach those challenges with a sense of confidence when they came along.

Because my search for Sophie had become such a hot topic

throughout my counseling sessions, I was anxious for Olivia to meet my 'mystery woman,' to see and hear what I had so often described to her, and to reveal what had remained hidden for so very long behind the veil of an unsettling dream. After explaining my reasons to Sophie, she agreed to meet me at the Green Gardens facility the very next day for my scheduled appointment.

Once inside, and after proper introductions, we seated ourselves in Olivia's office. For just a moment she looked over at us with both a look of surprise and just maybe a smile of relief, an acknowledgment of a struggle and search that had finally come to an end.

Olivia finally broke the silence, shaking her head in amazement as she spoke.

"Wow. Mike, do you realize when you told me about Sophie, when you described her, that you left an impression on me as well? When I saw you out there, Sophie, standing there with Mike, I knew it could be no one else. And so, we finally meet. Don't leave me in suspense, how did this all happen?"

We both shared our part in this incredible reunion, but I let Sophie take charge as I wanted Olivia to hear the voice, the lovely accent that I had described in detail for so long.

After hearing our story, Olivia stared back in amazement.

"I can't believe it. You two have made me a believer in destiny. I could have never imagined anything like this."

It was at this point that Olivia asked my permission to share one thought with Sophie. As always, her words were meaningful, thoughtful, and stated with purpose.

"When Mike first came to me, it was clear he had experienced an event of sorts that oddly left him with a memory of a lovely young woman he could not recall in his conscious world. I wanted you to hear this from me, because he was relentless, painfully relentless in trying to remember what his accident had taken from him.

More than anything, he wanted to remember, to find you, to just understand who you were and how you had met, and I hope I don't speak out of turn, but his memories of you were so full of warmth and comfort. When you originally met Mike, you clearly left him a gift, a part of yourself, something that would not allow his brain to forget. And you know, sometimes in life, the briefest of encounters can have the biggest impact on us."

We said our goodbyes to Olivia, but not before she and I mapped out a few last appointments. Olivia had become a voice of reason, the one person who pushed me and forced me to move outside of my comfort zone, challenging me to face my past, to embrace change, and to simply start living again. I would always be appreciative of all that she had done for me.

Once outside, Sophie walked over and hugged me. This day had been full of anticipation, emotion, and a genuine sense of renewal. As we walked away together, I felt relief and a sense of anticipation for this new-found friendship.

20

Life always has a bit of uncertainty sprinkled about it at times, and early on I was careful not to have expectations with regards to my relationship with Sophie. There was no way to know where it might lead, or indeed if it would lead anywhere, yet I was certain that I had discovered a trusting friend, somebody who was willing to share, listen, laugh, and simply enjoy the adventure of living.

What I did know for certain, was that the frustrating and agonizing journey that resulted from a bewildering and mixed-up dream had finally come to an end, and how grateful I was for those two incredible moments of providence that occurred only by the narrowest of margins. This beautiful woman, once nothing but an image in an erratic and confusing narrative, had walked into my life once again, in the same café, and under what I can assume were very similar circumstances. Destiny had done its job.

The time had come to share this discovery with my family and the few others that I considered friends. When we made it to Flynn and Emily's house, it was as comical as it was dramatic in some sense. We both were witness to the two of them staring in amazement and disbelief at this dream girl who stood before them in the flesh, and when the initial shock of meeting Sophie had quelled somewhat, there were hugs to be shared and a story to be told. My video call to Chicago, with Sophie at my side, yielded similar results.

The exclamations of surprise and the barrage of questions, and even a few tears running down the faces of my mother and Robyn, made me realize just how much this very longy and strenuous journey had impacted upon my own family.

I had one last video call to make, and it was to my French comrade Antoine, who never forgot my search, helping me however he could. Once connected, and after some head-shaking on Antoine's part, there was that story to be told again, and questions to be answered. After expressing his thoughts about our incredible encounter with destiny, and before we said our goodbyes, Antoine was determined to remind me of something he had shared with me when we first met.

"Remember what I told you long ago—that the most beautiful women in the world are French. Well, there is the very proof sitting right next to you."

Afterward, as we sat together in my apartment, Sophie's eyes fell upon the small, framed snapdragon note—and as she lifted it from the end table, I could sense a change in her mood as she cradled it gently in her hands.

"I'm so sorry what happened to you. When you found this note, it must have been tortuous."

For a few moments afterward she held on to me tightly, offering me comfort, much like she had done in my long and puzzling dream. I assured her all was okay, an unfortunate accident, but I had no desire to wallow in the aftermath of this event. What was done was done, and it was time to look ahead now, to move away from all those past moments and events that had followed me for so very long.

DAYS LATER, SOPHIE CAME to my apartment, the result of a dinner invitation, with me as the chef and her as the hungry guest. Despite her insistence on helping in the kitchen, I finally asserted myself, providing her with drinks and a small starter as she relaxed on the sofa. Our relationship in these early days had proceeded carefully and, respecting each other's pasts, neither of us wanted to fall prey to any errors of judgment. It was clear our lives had become interconnected, but neither of us wanted to jeopardize what felt like a very promising relationship.

That being said, and despite our reservations, these two friends soon became lovers. As we embraced, we had each overcome our own fears and were learning to trust again and discover the value of reaching out and being a part of something much more significant and meaningful.

Sophie's own story was resurrected later in the evening, when she spoke of her past relationship with her ex-partner, Victor. Her own story, like mine, had elements of sadness and regret, but his decision to leave her had struck her down, having to pick up the pieces of her life and move on. Sophie described him as a selfish man, even cruel at times, and she found herself living his life and not her own. Eventually he found his escape in the arms of another woman, and simply told Sophie he didn't love her anymore.

After hearing her story, I understood that maybe Sophie had been crossing a rickety bridge of her own and was, like me, stuck somewhere in the middle, unsure as to how best to proceed. I figured that sometimes it takes being out there on that bridge to recognize others who are also struggling with challenging journeys of their own. During those times, none of us can really know what awaits us on the other side of that bridge. Maybe in some ways, we create our own outcomes by the choices we make, and what is out there on either end of that bridge is of our own making. I'm glad that Sophie and I found one another out there in the vastness of life, as we ventured along paths unknown. Destiny brought us together, and now, just possibly, similar life journeys have united us.

It all made sense.

DECEMBER WAS ONE OF my favorite times of the year, with Christmas on the way and all the lights, decorations, and the buzz of the season all around. I used to love this time of year and the celebratory distraction that the holidays always provided. I remember so many Christmases past, as I sat with my parents and sister in our family living room, eating freshly baked cookies, and watching holiday movies on the television. It was a family event, decorating our tree and home together, with my father untangling the lights pulled from their hiding place amongst one of the many boxes stored away in the attic, and my mother carefully unwrapping her cherished decorations, telling stories as to the history of each bulb, candle, or holiday character as she went along.

On one clear and crisp weeknight just before Christmas, Sophie and I walked through London, watching the shoppers scurrying in and out of the shops, restaurants, and pubs. We walked along Oxford Street, enjoying the Christmas lights and colorful displays along the way, finally making our way to Covent Garden where we treated ourselves to some mulled wine to warm ourselves up. Eventually we wandered into one of the many restaurants in the area to rest our weary legs, warm our hands, and treat ourselves to a tasty meal.

When my father died and I moved from Chicago, that spirit and anticipation of the Christmas season slowly diminished within me, and I often found myself wandering the London streets on my own, wondering if that sense of holiday cheer would ever return. But enter Sophie, and for the first time in years, the Christmas season came alive for me again, as we marveled at the simple pleasures of sparkling lights and the sound of bells and Christmas music emanating so magically throughout the streets. Sophie and I even shopped for a tabletop Christmas tree and decorations, including tinsel and colored lights, and spent one very enjoyable evening fully adorning my tree and apartment, finally reawakening within me the spirit of Christmases past.

WHEN CHRISTMAS HAD COME and gone, Sophie and I made our way over to France for a New Year's gathering at her parents' home. I had already met Paul and Simone Allemand, along with Sophie's sister Josette, when they came for a weekend visit to London, which took some of the pressure off. Aunts, uncles, friends, and neighbors were all there to welcome in the New Year at the stroke of midnight, and despite my naturally hesitant nature when it came to larger social events, the music, drink, and rather raucous celebrations were wonderful to behold. I felt a sense of comfort within the home, being so warmly welcomed by Sophie's parents, and extended family and friends, even though many didn't speak English.

It was an odd feeling, finding myself immersed in the French culture, and watching on with fondness as Sophie hugged her parents and family members, celebrating these small yet significant life moments. Sitting there, being witness to that celebration of life, made me realize how much I had cast aside and abandoned such moments, in favor of a life absent of substance and personal connection. However, on that night, I celebrated with these people, Sophie's tribe, her loved ones—all of whom came together on one special occasion to participate in the joyous dance of life, and share in the simple pleasure of togetherness.

DURING THE SECOND WEEK of January, I stood alongside Sophie in church and observed the baptism of Elizabeth Adelaide Warner. As I watched and listened to the proceedings, celebrating along with Flynn and Emily as they shared this life event with family and friends, I found myself thinking back to a time when my own Catholic faith had been a notable part of my life. My parents were ardent Catholics and attending Mass was a family event for us, a time each week when we would stand together and share in the solemn convention of professing our faith.

When I left home and started my life as a young adult, church attendance dropped quite low on my list of things to do. I never lost my faith, but I struggled with having to stand in a crowded church attempting to reflect upon the mysteries of my religion, surrounded by crying babies and enduring long, rambling sermons. As I got older, I would sometimes make my way to my local church at a time during the day when the church would be empty and dimly lit, and sit and pray in silence, relishing the hushed and peaceful surroundings of this private sanctuary.

When my father died, I remember standing at his funeral service trying to reconcile such a pointless death, and for so long after, struggling with the confusion as to why this senseless tragedy would have befallen such an honorable and caring person. Eventually, I began to struggle with my own guilt, but also anger, with much of it directed at the man who had murdered my father, to the point that it tore at me and left me floundering to find any relief.

Despite her best efforts, my mother knew I would struggle with guilt for some time, once telling me that she didn't know how to undo that sense of self-blame that I was feeling. However, the three of us did talk about forgiveness. My mother said my father would not have wanted any of us to lead a life where we could not forgive and move on. Instead, he would have wanted us to liberate ourselves from any hate and destructive thinking—only accomplishing this through forgiveness.

My mother was a gallant role model to both Robyn and me during those times, and she never lost her direction in life because of what happened to my father. Each Sunday, she continued to go to church and profess her faith, and always strived to be the best person she could be. I was able to let go of some of the hate I felt in my heart, but liberation would be a long way off for me—finding forgiveness for someone else's behavior or actions is one thing, but being able to forgive yourself is something entirely different.

When I sat in empty, dimly lit churches, I would often think of my father and remember him for the brilliant man he was. Like so many children, I wanted my father to like what his son had become, but trying to understand what he thought and how he felt was difficult for me to imagine. So, I put my guilt in that backpack of mine and carried it around with me for so very long, becoming my burden, my reminder of a son who failed to reach out to his father, maybe when he needed me the most.

As the proceedings carried on in front of us, I felt Sophie grab my hand and hold it, refocusing my attention upon Flynn and Emily as they stood proudly in front of family and friends, professing their own faith and affirming their role and commitment as Christian parents. It was at that moment that I was reminded of my own faith, that incredible act of believing in something or someone, void of proof or expectations, yet having total confidence and conviction that your beliefs are valid and meaningful. My father's death had torn me down, and in the process made me question my faith. Thankfully, this brief celebration had proved refreshing, and as Sophie and I walked from the church, I was reminded of my long journey back, confident that those times of incredulity had now come to pass.

Our January ended with a trip to Chicago to share in a late holiday celebration with my family. It was Christmas all over again, and the opportunity for Sophie to meet family and integrate herself into the American way of life. Our arrival in Chicago was both exciting and somewhat comical, as my mother and Robyn's continuing fascination with the mysterious Sophie was finally brought to life as they shared hugs and kisses, bombarding her with yet more questions on the way home from the airport.

Our visit to Chicago was brilliant, and as I watched Sophie share in our lives, I recognized that all of us had been transformed in some respect. In the short time since we met, both Sophie and I had become a part of something much bigger than our own relationship, merging our lives with each other's families, entering this new territory with both excitement and anticipation. Our belated Christmas and New Year's dinner proved to be a grand celebration for many reasons, including Sophie's place at the family table and the return of some lost family traditions.

One cold night, the entire family walked the downtown streets of Chicago, reveling in the winter cityscape, before making our way to my mother's favorite eatery for some of the city's finest pizza. That night at home, we sat and enjoyed the warmth of a gas fireplace, played games, told stories, and laughed and danced together, as some of Robyn's favorite tunes played in the background. And as our small but joyous festivities continued, I glanced about the room and was thankful that I had rediscovered my family again, appreciative of their perseverance and tolerance, as they patiently awaited the return of a wayward soul.

AFTER MONTHS OF FINDING our way together, I finally packed up my belongings, said goodbye to my Greenwich apartment, and moved into Sophie's West London residence. It was the beginning of April and with the feel of spring in the air, our life together as live-in partners had begun in earnest. As expected, we planted our garden, filling it with beautiful plants and flowers of all sorts, with the small and very colorful snapdragon patch becoming my favorite and most meaningful section of all.

In keeping with the theme, the framed note found its spot on the mantle above Sophie's quaint electric fire. The mantle would eventually become a resting ground for all sorts of oddities that would remind us of our ongoing journey together, with only very special and noteworthy items finding their way into the mix. Yet the simple snapdragon note, so elegantly scripted by Sophie, stood out above the rest—reminding us of the beautiful gift of destiny that had smiled down upon us, not once, but twice.

In early June, I surprised Sophie with a weekend trip to Nice, where we walked the streets of the city, shopping at the Cours Saleya market and more importantly strolling through the lanes of the old town, as we made our way to my memorable restaurant in Garibaldi Square, La Fleur Bleue. Sitting there under the warm sun and having an afternoon drink together allowed me to celebrate that moment, ridding myself of memories and agonizing searches that had ended in disappointment and yet more unanswered questions.

That evening, Sophie and I paid a visit to my friend Antoine, where we met his girlfriend and the wonder cat Brigitte. As we sat and reminisced, I thought of my determined quest way back when, as I wandered through the streets of Nice in a desperate attempt to discover both the woman of my dreams, and a long-awaited sense of redemption.

In the morning, Sophie and I walked along the Promenade,

around the market stalls of Cours Saleya, and again down to Garibaldi Square where we sat outside of La Fleur Bleue, basking in the warm sun, eating our tasty croissants, and just appreciating the day. It had been a simple, yet meaningful trip back to a place where I had visited while in a dream, remembering a beautiful young woman who came to me and kindly asked if I would watch over her colorful, cherished snapdragons.

Life is often scattered with uncertainties and when Sophie and I met, there were no expectations of what would happen, nor where things would lead. As our relationship grew and began to flourish, marriage never really crossed my mind. We became the best of friends and partners, and as our lives moved on with promise and anticipation, we discussed our future together—the reality of leaving our jobs for the countryside or small-town living, having children or not, our hopes and aspirations, and what life was to become for us as a couple.

Neither Sophie nor I spoke about marriage, other than an occasional passing reference, and I didn't want to marry for any of the wrong reasons, and I was sure Sophie felt the very same. We had been a couple for almost nine months, and during that time, I discovered the beauty of our relationship, a deep commitment to each other and a love and fulfillment that was greater than anything I had ever experienced in my life. So, why formalize it?

But one incredible day, as Sophie and I were painting the walls of our bedroom, laughing at the very messy outcome of a rather spontaneous and unexpected paint war, I heard life calling out to me in such a purposeful way. Maybe now it was our turn to step up and take this opportunity to create our own story together.

So, on one glorious day at the end of August, Sophie and I headed to the West End to wander around, as per my request, finding our way to the Open House Café near Drury Lane, where we had first met. Once settled in and with very little fanfare, I asked Sophie if she would marry me, apologizing for not getting down on one knee or proposing under some exotic waterfall.

The smile on her face pretty much said it all, and with absolute calmness in her voice, she simply said, "Yes Mike, of course I will marry you. My love, this day, this place, it was all perfect. Nothing else could have compared."

As it was, Sophie had been waiting for me to ask her—she knew it was coming, she told me, and on that day as we walked from the Open House, another chapter in our life was about to be written.

SOPHIE AND I WERE married on the 20th of October in a small church not far from her parents' house. It was a Friday evening wedding, and our small but lively reception took place at an intimate venue in the countryside, before our small wedding party—families and close friends—continued the celebration at Sophie's parents' home later that night. This marriage had become more than a union of just two people, it had become a unique blend of family and friends who were now joined together because of us. My life was no longer solitary—I was a husband, an in-law and had a network of French relatives. My world had indeed changed, and on that night of celebration, as Sophie and I stood amidst both of our families and close friends, I felt thankful again for all that life had given to me.

When I look back at my life in retrospect, it was sadly evident that I had found it all too easy to live by the negative messages I had given myself, feeling unworthy of anything better or deserving. Those messages became a self-fulfilling prophecy, forcing me into a life of routine, going through the motions of living without really experiencing it all, and in the process losing my passion, sense of intimacy, and ability to connect with those around me—including my own family. I had become stuck in a loop, burdened with haunting memories that pounded at me relentlessly, only finding my escape by adapting to life on the run. It was easier, safer, and without complication, finding my own respite through routine and isolation. I went into exile, stranded and with little hope of finding my way back.

I became invisible in a visible world, hiding myself away within the vacant spaces of life.

It was only when life offered me salvation as the result of an unfortunate accident that I found the determination and willingness to step away from an aimless existence, and begin the process of seeking change. As part of this redemptive process, I was finally able to forgive myself for not being there with my father on that fateful day, allowing me to break free from the confines of a very small, closed-off world.

After that very lengthy and difficult exile, giving myself permission to seek out a new life, I managed to find my way out of the maze that I created and existed in for such a long time and opened my world to others, transforming my life in a meaningful manner.

In the end, this story of chance and discovery more than likely would not have happened if I had remained stuck in the middle of my analogous rickety bridge. Only when I faced up to the guilt, grief, and anger that had rendered me motionless and kept me disconnected and isolated from those around me, was I able to build my resources, restore within me all that had been damaged and disregarded, and finally get moving along that rickety bridge.

Not long after we were married, Sophie asked me if I would write our story, to put into words the experiences and circumstances of our past that would eventually serve as the catalyst for the fascinating adventure that would bring us together. She felt that this incredible set of events and fantastical experience was a story worth telling. So, in the end it was Sophie, my mystery figure of long past, and now my lovely wife, who asked me to tell this tale, because, as she simply stated, "As wild and mixed-up as this journey had been, it's definitely a story to be told."

On those occasions when Sophie and I would talk of our future together, we were certainly aware of all that life could deliver, both good and otherwise, and we knew without a doubt that this beautiful and sometimes messy journey of life would be a risk worth taking. Destiny had kindly brought us together, and with this incredible path of life outstretched in front of us, we knew for certain that those adventures of living were out there, waiting patiently for us to make the first move.

AFTERWORD

Daylight has broken. The morning dew glistens and sparkles upon the sunlit surface as I stride through neighborhoods awakening to the new day. The air is cool, refreshing me as I wind my way through familiar streets, with the light of the early morning sun seemingly leading me onward as I run by sleepy homes roused to life by the new dawn breaking.

Today as I run, I am liberated from the darkness, which once protected me and offered me refuge from the peering eyes of society and those occupants who often sought me out. I run now without self-imposing rules and boundaries, all of which kept me distant and detached from the smiles and outstretched hands of others.

As I run on without restraint or burden upon me, the path ahead silently beckons me forward, offering comfort and respite from the urgency of the often-demanding world and all its dictates. I no longer seek isolation, but instead enjoy the pleasure of being one of the participants, visible and available to share in the experience of living. The heavy burden of an unresolved past and all its self-destructive messages has now been lifted. I have knocked down the walls of my prison and danced upon its ruins, leaving the smashed remnants behind me as I make my way homeward. I have freed myself. I am liberated.

Today, the most rewarding thing of all, is that I run alongside my beautiful life partner. Our footsteps and our rhythmic breathing are pleasantly accompanied by our laughter and chatter as we make our way together on this carefree journey. We have no agenda, no set pace, no expectations, and we run until we choose to stop.

As we walk back home together, hand-in-hand, we stop for a moment and hug one another as the morning sun bathes us in its warm sunshine. We have arrived, and in that moment, we hold each other tight, and are thankful for what this world and this life together has given us.

And as we walk on, we smile at one another, because we know with certainty, that today is going to be a beautiful day.

ACKNOWLEDGMENTS

From a very young age, the desire to create a story and make it come to life in the form of a completed novel, remained nothing more than some flight of fancy, a wishful indulgence of a 'wannabe writer.' How many times I started this journey and quit along the way – it just became the easy thing to do. Despite having the desire to write and create, I repeatedly told myself that if I did attempt this undertaking, it would more than likely end with all efforts wasted, accompanied by pages of unfinished thoughts and ideas sitting idle – eventually fading away with time, never to be revisited.

Yet somehow, I never let go of that wishful thought, and so I persisted, and after decades of start and stop, and periods of inactivity, I began that journey once again, pushing onward the best I could. When I finished this story, the satisfaction and acknowledgement that this long held aspiration had finally come to fruition, was the only outcome needed. However, this journey would not have been completed without the support and intervention of those very special few who offered me so much encouragement along the way. And so…

My special thanks and deepest appreciation to my editor, Dominic Wakeford, for his 'long-standing' support throughout this entire project. Dom's expertise, professionalism, and his incredible level of commitment has been commendable. It would have been easy to lose my way without Dom's steady guidance, and when moments of self-doubt would in turn lead to frustration, his generous words of encouragement would help me re-focus and find my balance once again. It must be said that Dom's incredible level of tolerance was a significant factor in managing the development of the manuscript, as on many an occasion, my resistance to editorial recommendations and change could be quite an entrenched shortcoming. It didn't take me long to realize that Dom's role was both skillful and technical, and that his attention to detail eventually allowed me to re-shape the manuscript into a more concise and meaningful story. Above all, Dom approached my project in a sensitive manner, always ensuring that my work and efforts were valued, and that a successful and timely outcome remained a priority. For all of Dom's passion towards my project, I am most grateful. I couldn't have completed this journey without his brilliant collaboration and support.

My thanks also to Vanessa Mendozzi, book designer and typesetting specialist, for her creative concepts and most valuable contributions to the final project. Vanessa's creativity and vision, allowed for a strong visual concept to be introduced into the project, one that created a connecting 'bridge' between imagery and the written word. Her expertise, technical skill and organized approached was critical in bringing this project to its conclusion. Thanks to Vanessa for listening to my thoughts on the project and for helping to bring the necessary structure and finishing touch to the final product.

A gracious thank you to my loving wife Lorraine, for her unending support, patience and her unwavering commitment in helping me to achieve this outcome. Lorraine's role as an avid reader proved to be a valuable resource, as her ongoing review and constructive approach to the manuscript helped me along the way to rewrite and modify specific aspects of the story. I am grateful to Lorraine's encouragement and her willingness to stand-by and endure my moments of frustration. Throughout this very long and at times challenging undertaking, Lorraine continued to inspire me and always made the time to listen and discuss, all the while providing me the needed push when necessary. So, a very special thanks to this beautiful woman and my best friend, who continued to walk alongside me until the journey's end.

Lastly, my deepest appreciation to all those family and friends who have supported and encouraged me along the way. Your kind words will live on forever. Thank you so much.

JM

www.ingramcontent.com/pod-product-compliance
Lightning Source LLC
Chambersburg PA
CBHW022127050726
47590CB00002B/449